DARK HORSE

////

J.R. RAIN

JIM KNIGHTHORSE SERIES

Dark Horse
The Mummy Case
Hail Mary
Clean Slate
Night Run
Easy Rider (short story)

Published by
Crop Circle Books
212 Third Crater, Moon

Printed in the United States of America.

ISBN: 9781720297840

1.

Charles Brown, the defense attorney, was a small man with a round head. He was wearing a brown and orange zigzagged power tie. I secretly wondered if he went by Charlie as a kid and had a dog named Snoopy and a crush on the little red-headed girl.

We were sitting in my office on a warm spring day. Charlie was here to give me a job if I wanted it, and I wanted it. I hadn't worked in two weeks and was beginning to like it, which made me nervous.

"I think the kid's innocent," he was saying.

"Of course you do, Charlie. You're a defense attorney. You would find cause to think Jack the Ripper was simply a misunderstood artist before his time."

He looked at me with what was supposed to be a stern face.

"The name's Charles," he said.

"If you say so."

"I do."

"Glad that's cleared up."

"I heard you could be difficult," he said. "Is this you being difficult? If so, then I'm disappointed."

I smiled. "Maybe you have me confused with my father."

Charlie sat back in my client chair and smiled. His domed head was perfectly buffed and polished, cleanly reflecting the halogen lighting above. His skin appeared wet and viscous, as if his sweat glands were ready to spring into action at a moment's notice.

"Your father has quite a reputation in L.A. I gave his office a call before coming here. Of course, he's quite busy and could not take on an extra case."

"So you settled on the next best thing."

"If you want to call it that," he said. "I've heard that you've performed adequately with similar cases, and so I've decided to give you a shot, although my expectations are not very high, and I have another P.I. waiting in the wings."

"How reassuring," I said.

"Yeah, well, he's established. You're not."

"But can he pick up a blind side blitz?"

Charlie smiled and splayed his stubby fingers flat on my desk and looked around my office, which was adorned with newspaper clippings and photographs of yours truly. Most of the photographs depict me in a Bruin uniform, sporting the number 45. In most I'm carrying the football, and in others I'm blowing open the hole for the tailback. Or at least I like to think I'm blowing open the hole. The newspapers are yellowing now, taped or tacked to the wood paneling. Maybe someday I'll take them down. But not yet.

"You beat SC a few years back. I can never forgive you for that. Two touchdowns in the fourth quarter alone."

"Three," I said. "But who's counting?"

He rubbed his chin. "Destroyed your leg, if I recall, in the last game of the season. Broken in seven different places."

"Nine, but who's counting?"

"Must have been hard to deal with. You were on your way to the pros. Would have made a hell of a fullback."

That *had* been hard to deal with, and I didn't feel like talking about it now to Charlie Brown. "Why do you believe in your client's innocence?" I asked.

He looked at me. "I see. You don't want to talk about it. Sorry I brought it up." He crossed his legs. He didn't seem sorry at all. He looked smugly down at his shoes, which had polish on the polish. "Because I believe Derrick's story. I believe he loved his girlfriend and would never kill her."

"People have been killed for love before. Nothing new."

On my computer screen before me I had brought up an article from the Orange County Register. The article showed a black teen being led away into a police car. He was looking down, his head partially covered by his jacket. He was being led away from a local high school. A very upscale high school, if I recalled. The story was dated three weeks ago, and I recalled reading it back then.

I tapped the computer monitor. "The police say there's some indication that his girlfriend was seeing someone else, and that jealousy might have been a factor."

"Yes," said the attorney. "And we think this someone else framed our client."

"I take it you want me to find this man."

"Or person."

"Ah, equality," I said.

"We want you to find evidence of our client's innocence, whether or not you find the true murderer."

"Anything else I should know?"

"We feel race might be a factor here. He was the only black student in school, and in the neighborhood."

"I believe the preferred term is African-American."

"I'm aware of public sentiment in this regards. I don't need you to lecture me."

"Just trying to live up to my difficult name."

"Yeah, well, cool it," he said. "Now, no one's talking at the school. My client says he was working out late in the school gym, yet no one saw him, not even the janitors."

"Then maybe he wasn't there."

"He was there," said Charlie simply, as if his word was enough. "So do you want the job?"

"Sure."

We discussed a retainer fee and then he wrote me a check. When he left, waddling out of the office, I could almost hear Schroeder playing on his little piano in the background.

J.R. RAIN

2.

"He was found with the murder weapon," said Detective Hanson. "It was in the backseat of his car. That's damning evidence."

"That," I said, "and he's black."

"And he's black," said Hanson.

"In an all white school," I said.

"Yep."

"Were his prints on the knife?"

"No."

We were sitting in an outdoor café facing the beach. It was spring, and in southern California that's as good as summer. Many underdressed women were roller-blading, jogging or walking their dogs on the narrow beach path. There were also some men, all finely chiseled, but they were not as interesting.

Detective Hanson was a big man, but not as big as me. He had neat brown hair parted down the middle. His thick mustache screamed cop. He wore slacks and a white shirt. He was sweating through his shirt. I was dressed in khaki shorts, a surfing T-shirt and white Vans. Coupled with my amazing tan and disarming smile, I was surprised I wasn't more often confused with Jimmy Buffet. If Jimmy Buffet stood six foot four and weighed two hundred and twenty.

"You guys have anything else on the kid?" I asked.

"You know I can't divulge that. Trial hasn't even started. The info about the knife made it to the press long ago, so that's a freebie for you. I can tell you this: the body was found at one a.m., although the ME places the time of death around seven p.m. the previous night."

"Who found the body?"

"A neighbor."

"Where were the victim's parents?"

"Dinner and dancing. It was a Friday night."

"Of course," I said. "Who doesn't go out and dance on a Friday night?"

"I don't," said Hanson.

"Me neither," I said. "Does Derrick have an alibi?"

"This will cost you a tunacoda."

"You drive a hard bargain."

I called the waitress over and put in our lunch orders.

"No alibi," Hanson said when she had left, "but...." He let his voice trail off.

"But you believe the kid?"

He shrugged. "Yeah. He seems like a good kid. Says he was working out at the school gym at the time."

"Schools have janitors, staff, students."

"Yeah, well, it was late and no one saw him."

"Or no one chose to see him."

Hanson shrugged.

Our food arrived. A tunacoda for the detective. A half pound burger for me, with grilled onions and cheese, and a milkshake.

"You trying to commit suicide?" he asked.

"I'm bulking up," I said.

"This is how you bulk up? Eating crap?"

"Only way I know how."

"Why?"

"Thinking of trying out for San Diego," I said.

"The Chargers?"

"Yeah."

"What about your leg?"

"The leg's going to be a problem."

He thought about that, working his way through his tuna and avocado sandwich. He took a sip from his Coke.

"You wanna bash heads with other men and snap each other in the shower with jock straps, go right ahead."

"It's not as glamorous as that."

"Suicide, I say. What's your dad think?"

"He doesn't know. You're the first person I've told."

"I'm honored."

"You should be."

"What's Cindy going to say?"

I sipped my milkshake. "She won't like it, but she will support me. She happens to think very highly of me and my decisions."

He snorted and finished his sandwich, grabbed his Styrofoam cup.

"I can't believe I was bribed with a shitty tuna sandwich and a Coke."

"A simple man with simple needs."

"I should resent that remark, if it wasn't so true." He stood. "I gotta run. Good luck with the kid, but I think it's a lost cause. Kid even has a record."

"What kind?"

"Vandalism, mostly. He's a goner. Hear they're gonna try him as an adult."

Detective Hanson left with his Styrofoam cup. I noticed he wasn't wearing socks. Even cops in Huntington Beach are cool.

J.R. RAIN

3.

Cindy Darwin is an anthropology professor at UCI.

Her expertise is in the anthropology of religion, which, she tells me, is an important aspect of anthropology. And, yes, she can trace her lineage back to Charles Darwin, which makes her a sort of icon in her field. She knows more things about anthropology than she probably should, and too few things about the real world. Maybe that's why she keeps me around.

It was late and we were walking hand-in-hand along the Huntington Pier. From here we could see the lights of Catalina Island, where the reclusive sorts live and travel via ferry and plane. To the north, in the far distance, we could see Long Beach glittering away. The air was cool and windy and we were dressed in light jackets and jeans. Her jeans were much snugger and more form-fitting than mine. As they should be.

"I'm thinking of giving San Diego a call," I said.

"Who's in San Diego?" she asked. She had a slightly higher pitched voice than most women. I found it endlessly sexy. She said her voice made it easier to holler across an assembly hall. Gave it more range, or something.

I was silent. She put two and two together. She let go of my hand.

"They call you again?" she asked. "The Rams, right?"

"The Chargers. Christ, Cindy, your own brother plays on the team."

"I think it's all sort of silly. Football, I mean. And all those silly mascots, I just don't get it."

"The mascots help us boys tell the teams apart," I said. "And, no, they didn't call. But I'm thinking about their last offer."

"Honey, that was two years ago."

She was right. I turned them down two years

ago. My leg hadn't felt strong enough.

"The leg's better now," I said.

"Bullshit. You still limp."

"Not as much. And when I workout, I feel the strength again."

"But you still have metal pins in it."

"Lots of players play with pins."

"Have you told Rob yet?" she asked. Rob was her brother, the Chargers fourth wide receiver. Rob had introduced me to Cindy during college.

"Yes."

"What does he think?"

"He thinks it's a good idea."

We stopped walking and leaned over the heavy wooden rail. The air was suffused with brine and salt. Waves crashed beneath us, white-caps glowing in the moonlight. A lifeguard Jeep was parked next to us, a quarter into the ocean on the pier. All that extra weight on the pier made me nervous.

"Why now?" she asked finally.

"My window is rapidly closing," I said.

"Not to mention you've always wondered if you could do it."

"Not to mention."

"And you're frustrated out of your gourd that a fucking leg injury has prevented you from finding this out."

"Such language from an anthropologist."

She sighed and hugged me around my waist. She was exactly a foot shorter than me, which made hugging easy, and kissing difficult.

"So what do you think?" I asked.

"I think you're frustrated and angry and that you need to do this."

"Not to mention I might just make a hell of a fullback."

"Is he the one who throws the ball?"

We had gone over this precisely one hundred and two times.

"No, but close."

She snuggled closer, burying her sharp chin deep into my side. It tickled. If I wasn't so tough I would have laughed.

"Just don't get yourself hurt."

"I don't plan to, but these things have a way of taking you by surprise."

"So are you really that good?" she asked, looking up at me.

"I'm going to find out."

She looked away. "If you make the team, things will change."

I hugged her tighter. "I know."

4.

I was in a conference room at the Orange County jail in Santa Ana, accompanied by Charley Brown's assistant, Mary Cho.

We were alone, waiting for Derrick Booker to make his grand appearance. Mary was Chinese and petite and pretty. She wore a blue power suit, with the hem just above her knees. She sat next to me, and from our close proximity I had a clear view of her knees. Nice knees. Cho was probably still a law student. Probably worked out a whole lot. Seemed a little uptight, but nothing a little alcohol couldn't fix. Was probably a little tigress in bed. She wasn't much of a talker and seemed immune to my considerable charm. Probably because she had caught me looking at her knees.

The heavy door with the wire window opened and Derrick was shown into the conference room by two strapping wardens. He was left alone with us, the wardens waiting just outside the door. The kid himself was manacled and hogtied. Should he make a run for it, Pope John Paul II himself could have caught him from behind.

Mary Cho sprang to life, brightening considerably, leaning forward and gesturing to a chair opposite us.

"Derrick, thanks for meeting us," she said.

He shrugged, raising his cuffed hands slightly. "As if I had anything better to do."

Which is what I would have said. I stifled a grin. I suspected grins were illegal in the Orange County jail. Derrick sounded white, although he tried to hide that fact with a lot of swaggering showmanship. In fact, he sounded white *and* rich, with a slightly arrogant lilt to his voice. He was good looking, with strong features and light brown eyes. He was tall and built like an athlete.

"I have someone here who wants to speak

with you," said Cho.

"Who? Whitey?"

I raised my hand. "That would be me."

Derrick's father owned lots of real estate across southern California, and Derrick himself had grown up filthy rich. He was about as far from the ghetto as you could get. Yet here he was, sounding as if he had lived the mean streets all his life. As if he had grown up in poverty, rather than experiencing the best Orange County had to offer, which is considerable. I suspected here in prison he was in survival mode, where being a wealthy black kid is as bad as being a wealthy white kid. Except that he had the jargon wrong and a few years out of date, and he still sounded upper class, no matter how hard he tried to hide it.

"My name's Jim Knighthorse."

"Hey, I know you, man!"

"Who doesn't?" I said. "And those who don't, should."

He smiled, showing a row of perfect white teeth. "How's your leg? Saw you bust it up against Miami. Hell, I wanted to throw up."

"I did throw up. You play?"

"Yeah. Running back."

"You any good?" I asked.

"School is full of whities, what do you think?"

I shrugged. "Some whities can run."

He grinned again. "Yeah, no shit. You could run, bro. Dad says wasn't for your leg you'd be in the pros."

"Still might."

"No shit?"

"No shit."

"What about the leg?" he asked.

"We'll see about the leg," I said.

We were silent. Derrick was losing the ghetto speak. His eyes had brightened considerably with the football talk. We looked at each other. Down to business.

"You do her, Derrick?"

"Do her?"

"He means kill her, Derrick," said Cho. "He's asking if you killed Amanda Peterson."

"Thank you, assistant Cho," I said, smiling at her. She looked away quickly. Clearly she didn't trust herself around me. I looked back at Derrick. "You kill her, Derrick?"

"Hell, no."

His arms flexed. Bulbous veins stood out against his forearms, disappearing up the short sleeves of his white prison attire. I could see those arms carrying a football.

"Why should anyone believe you?" I asked.

"Give a fuck what anyone believes."

"They found the knife in your car, Derrick.

Her blood was on the knife. It adds up."

He was trying for hostile bad-ass, but he was just a kid, and eventually his emotions won out. They rippled across his expressive face, brief glimpses into his psyche: disbelief, rage, frustration. But most of all I saw *sorrow*. Deep sorrow.

"Because... " He stopped, swallowed, looked away. "Because we were going to get married."

"Married?"

"Uh huh."

"How old are you?"

"Seventeen."

"How old was she?"

"The same."

"Anyone know about the marriage?" I asked.

He laughed hollowly. "Hell, no. Her dad hates me, and I'm sure he doesn't think much of me now."

"I wouldn't imagine he does," I said. "You have any theories who might have killed her?"

He hesitated. "No."

"Was she seeing anyone else?"

"No."

"You were exclusive?"

"Yes."

"How do you know?"

"She loved me."

"Did you love her?" I asked.

He didn't answer immediately. The silence that followed was palpable. The ticking of the clock behind us accentuated the silence and gave it depth and profundity. I listened to him breathe through his mouth. The corners of his mouth were flecked with dried spittle.

"Yeah, I loved her," he said finally. He swiped his sleeve across his face, using a shrugging motion to compensate for his cuffed wrists. The sleeve was streaked with tears.

"That will be enough, Mr. Knighthorse," said Cho. "Thank you, Derrick."

She got up and went to the door. She knocked on the window and the two wardens entered and led the shuffling Derrick out of the room. He didn't look back. I got up and stood by the door with Cho.

"What do you think?" she asked.

"I think you're secretly in love with me," I said.

"I think you're secretly in love with your-self."

"It's no secret," I said.

We left the conference room and moved down the purposefully bare-walled hallway. Perhaps colorful paintings would have given the accused false hope.

"The kid didn't do her," I said. "No one's

that good an actor."

She nodded. "We know. He's going to need your help."

"He's going to need a lot of help," I said.

"Let me guess: and you're the man to do it?"

"Took the words right out of my mouth."

5.

On Beach Blvd., not too far from my crime-fighting headquarters, there is a McDonald's fast food restaurant. McDonald's is a fairly well-known establishment here in Huntington Beach, California, although I can't vouch for the rest of the country since I don't get out much. This McDonald's features an epic two- or three-story plastic playground, an ATM and DVD rentals.

Oh, and it also features God.

Yes, God. The Creator. The Lord Of All That

Which Is And Is Not. The God of the Earth below and the sky above. The God of the Moon and the stars and Cher.

No, I'm not high. At least, not at the moment.

Oh, and he doesn't like me calling him God. He prefers Jack. Yes, Jack.

Again, I'm not high.

Let me explain: Not too long ago, while enjoying a Big Mac or three at this very Mc-Donald's, a homeless man dressed in rags and smelling of an overripe dumpster sat across from me. He introduced himself as God, and later, by my third Big Mac, I almost believed him.

God or not, he offered some pretty damn good advice that day, and I have been coming back ever since.

Today, by my second Big Mac and third refill of Coke, he showed up, ambling up to the restaurant from somewhere on Beach Blvd. Where he came from, I don't know. Where he goes, I still didn't know. Maybe Heaven. Maybe a dumpster. Maybe both.

As he cut across the parking lot, heading to the side entrance, I noted that his dirty jeans appeared particularly torn on this day. Perhaps he had had a fight with the Devil earlier.

Jack went through the door, walked up to the

cashier, ordered a coffee.

"Hi, Jim," he said, after he had gotten his coffee. He carefully lifted the lid with very dirty fingers and blew on the steaming brew.

"God doesn't like his coffee too hot?" I asked. I had been curious about this, as he always blew on his cups.

"No," he said simply. God, or Jack, was an average-sized man, with average features: His hair was of average color and length (neutral brown, hanging just above his ears), his eyes of average color (brownish, although they could have been green), and his skin was of average tone (perhaps Caucasian, although he could have passed for Hispanic). In short, the man was completely nondescript and nearly invisible to the world at large. He would make a hell of a P.I., actually.

Jack finally looked up from his coffee and studied me with his neutrally-colored eyes, squinting a little. I felt again that he was looking deep within me, into my heart and soul. While he was reading my aura, or whatever the hell it was he was doing, I looked down at his coffee: It was no longer steaming.

"How's your day going, Jim?" he finally asked me, sipping from the cup, using both hands, cradling the thing carefully, as if it were the Cup of Life.

He always asked me that, and I always said, which I did now: "Fine, Jack. How's it hanging?"

"Some would be offended to hear you speak to God in such an irreverent, disrespectful manner."

"Sure," I said. "Hell, I'm even offended. Can't you tell?"

He laughed softly.

"As they say, I broke the mold with you, Jim. And they're hanging to the left. They're always hanging to the left. Isn't there anything else you want to ask God?"

"Sure," I said. "For starters, how do I know you're God?"

We were mostly alone at the back of the seating area. Behind me, kids played in the massive two-story jungle gym. Such jungle gyms didn't exist when I was a kid. Lucky bastards.

"You have faith, Jim. That's how," he said. He always said that to me.

"How about for a lark you perform a miracle."

"You're alive and breathing," he said, sipping his coffee. "Isn't that miracle enough?"

"No," I said. "It's not, dammit." I was used to these kinds of double-talk answers. Jack seemed particularly efficient at this. "Make a million dollars appear. I don't even have to keep it. Just make it appear."

"And that would prove to you that I'm God?"

"Sure."

"Is it God you seek, or a genie?"

"Genie would be nice, too."

"I'll look into it."

"Thanks."

We were quiet. Jack silently sipped his coffee. Not even a slurp.

"You haven't been around for a while," he said.

"Have you missed me?"

"Yes."

"You have been waiting for me?" I asked, mildly shocked. It had been, perhaps, four months since I'd last visited with him.

"Yes," he said.

"How did you know I was here today?" I asked.

He grinned.

"There's something to be said for being omniscient, Jim."

"I bet," I said. "Anyway, I haven't worked on a case in a while. That is, a real case."

"You only come when you're working on a case?"

"Something like that," I said. "You would prefer I came more often?"

He looked at me from over his non-steaming cup of coffee.

"Yes," he said simply, and I found his answer oddly touching. "So am I to assume you are working on a case now?"

"You are God," I said. "You can assume anything you want."

"So is that a yes?"

I sighed.

"I'm working on a case, yes."

"Tell me about it."

"Don't you already know?" I asked. "Hell, don't you already know who killed the girl?"

He looked at me long and hard, unblinking, his face impassive. There was dirt in the corner of his eyes, and along the border of his scalp, where his roots met his forehead. He stank of something unknown and rotten and definitely foul.

You're insane, I told myself for the hundredth time. *Utterly insane to even remotely entertain the idea that this might be—*

"Yes," he said. "I do know who killed the girl."

My breath caught in my throat.

"Then tell me."

"You already know, my son."

We had discussed such matters before. Jack seemed to think I knew things that I didn't really know. He also seemed to think that time meant nothing to me and that I could sort of shift back and forth through it as I wished. I kindly let Jack know that I thought it all sounded like bullshit.

For now, I said, "I can assure you, Jack, that I most certainly do not know who killed her—and I most certainly do not want to get into that time-is-an-illusion horseshit, either. It makes my fucking head hurt, and you know it. Do you want to make my fucking head hurt, Jack?"

"Are you quite done?" he asked.

"Yes," I said, sitting back, taking a swig from my fourth or maybe fifth Coke.

He watched me quietly while I drank, then said, "Although you do know who killed the girl, but choose to deny the basic laws that govern your existence—in particular, time—I will give you the answer now if you so desire."

"Really?" I asked.

"Really."

"You know who killed Amanda Peterson?" I wasn't sure what my tone was: disbelief, curious, awe, maybe even a little fear. There are no secrets with God.

"Indeed," said Jack.

"But I haven't even discussed the case with you."

"I know."

"So why did you ask me to discuss the case with you?"

"It's called small talk, Jim. Try it sometime." And Jack winked at me.

I took in some air. These conversations were always like this. Circular. Infuriating. Often illuminating. Sometimes silly. But more often than not, just plain insane.

"Fine," I said, "write it down and I'll keep it in my wallet."

"Until?"

"Until the case is over. We'll see if we came to the same conclusions."

"Oh, we will."

"You're sure?"

"Always."

I often keep a pen above my ear, and as luck would have it, there was one there now. Jack tore off a piece of my tray liner, wrote something down on it, folded it up neatly and handed pen and paper to me. I deftly slipped the pen back over my ear, was briefly tempted to unfold the paper, but promptly shoved it in my wallet, behind an old condom.

"So how is Amanda?" I asked. Amanda being the murdered girl on my case, of course.

"She is happy."

"But she was slaughtered just a few weeks ago."

"Yes, but she is with me now."

"This is fucking weird," I said.

"It's as weird as you want it to be," said the bum in front of me. I saw that his coffee was nearly gone.

"Want another coffee?"

"Heavens, no. It'll keep me up all night."

"I thought God never sleeps."

He looked up at me and grinned, showing a row of coffee stained teeth.

"Why, whoever told you that?"

"I'll be back," I said. "And it won't be four months this time."

And as I left, sipping from my large plastic cup, I noticed for the first time the Monopoly guy on the side of the cup, holding in his fist a single million dollar bill.

I looked over at Jack, but he had gotten up and was currently talking with someone else, oblivious to me.

6.

Fresh from my conversation with God, I parked in front of a single story home with a copper roof, copper garage door and copper front door. I was sensing a pattern here. The front yard was immaculate and obviously prof-essionally maintained. Roses were perfectly pruned under the front bay windows. Thick bushes separated the house from its distant neighbor. The bushes were pruned into massive green balls.

In the center of the lawn was a pile of roses.

Mixed with the roses were teddy bears and cards and a massive poster with many signatures on it. The poster had photographs stapled to it. It was a sort of shrine to Amanda Peterson, marking the spot where she had been found murdered just forty-three days ago. The flowers themselves were in different stages of dying, and the grass around the shrine was trampled to death.

A lot of dying going on around here.

I let my car idle and studied the crime scene. The large round bushes could conceal anyone, an easy ambush point. There was only one street light in this cul-de-sac, and it was four houses down. Although upscale, the neighborhood had no apparent security. Anyone could have been waiting for her.

Anyone.

But probably not Derrick.

Then again, I've been wrong before.

According to the police report, a neighbor had been the first to discover the body. The first to call the cops. The first questioned. The neighbor claimed to have heard nothing, even while Amanda was being mutilated directly across the street. I wanted to talk to that neighbor.

I yanked a u-turn and parked across the street in front of a powder blue house. The house was huge and sprawling. And silent.

I rang the doorbell and waited. While doing so, I examined the distance from where Amanda was murdered to here. My internal judge of distance told me this: it wasn't that far.

No one answered. I utilized my backup plan and tried the doorbell again.

Nothing.

Plan C.

I strolled around the side of the house, reached over the side gate, unlatched the lock and walked into the backyard. As if I owned the place. Done with enough chutzpah and self-assurance that even the nosiest neighbor will hesitate to call the police. I was also fairly certain there was no dog, unless it was trained not to bark at the doorbell. Which few were.

In the backyard, pruning roses, was an older lady. She was dressed much younger and hipper than she probably was. She wore white Capri pants, a tank top, shades and tennis shoes. Her arms were tanned, the skin hanging loose. In Huntington Beach no one ages; or, rather, no one concedes to aging. Because she was armed with shearing knives, I kept my distance.

"Mrs. Dartmouth?" I asked pleasantly.

No response. More pruning.

I said her name louder and took a step closer. I was beginning to see how a murder could indeed happen across the street without her knowledge.

But then she finally turned and caught me out of the corner of her eye. She gasped and whipped the shearing knives around, ready to shear the hell out of me. Although thirty feet away, I stepped back, holding up my wallet and showing my private investigator license. A hell of a picture, I might add.

"Jim Knighthorse," I said. "Private investigator."

"Good Christ, you shouldn't sneak up on people around here, especially after what's happened."

"Yes, ma'am. I represent Carson and Deploma. I'd like to ask you a few questions."

She stood. "You're representing the boy?" she asked, her voice rising an octave. Not representing the *young man*. But the *boy*. She also sounded surprised, as if I were an idiot to do so.

"Yes."

She thought about that. She seemed to be struggling with something internally. Finally she shrugged.

"Would you like some iced tea?" she asked.

"Oh, would I."

At her patio table, she served it up with a mint sprig and a lemon wedge, and I suspected a dash or two of sugar. We were shaded by a green umbrella, and as Mrs. Dartmouth sat opposite me, I noticed the shears didn't stray far from her hand. Didn't blame her.

"Great tea."

"Should be. I put enough sugar in it."

She wore a lot of lipstick and smelled of good perfume. Her hair was in a tight bun, and she watched me coolly and maybe a little warily. Again, I didn't blame her. I was a big man. A big handsome, athletic and sensitive man.

"Have you talked to many people about Amanda's murder?" I asked.

She brightened. "Lordy, yes. Reporters, police, attorneys, everyone. I've been over it a hundred times."

She sounded as if she'd enjoy going over it a hundred more times, to anyone who would listen. Probably served a lot of this iced tea in the process. And the sugar kept them coming back for more.

"Well, I won't ask you anything that's not already on the police report."

"Fine."

"You knew Amanda personally?"

She nodded. "That poor dear. Such a sweet child."

"Did you know Derrick Booker?"

"No," she said. "He never dared show his face here. I understand that Mr. Peterson didn't take a liking to him."

"Were you aware of Amanda having any other boyfriends?"

"I wouldn't know. I'm not a nosy person."

I smiled at the lie. "Of course not. How well do you know the family?"

"I babysat Amanda when she was younger. But as she got older I saw less and less of her. They always forget about us old fogies."

"When was your last conversation with Amanda?"

She took a sip from her tea and watched me carefully. "Two years ago, when she was a freshman in high school, after she had quit the school marching band. She played an instrument. The flute, I think. She loved music."

"Why did she quit?"

"I hardly think this is relevant to her murder of a month and a half ago."

"Just fishing, ma'am. After all, like my dad says: you never know what you'll catch."

"Well, I do. They caught that boy. And that's good enough for me."

"It's good enough for a lot of people," I said. "Mrs. Dartmouth, what would you do if your daughter dated a black man?"

"What a silly question to ask."

"Why?"

"Because I don't have a daughter."

"I see," I said. "You were the first to come

across the body."

She swallowed. "Yes."

I waited a moment. "At one a.m."

"Yes. I was walking. I do that sometimes when I can't sleep."

"And at the time of the murder, you saw and heard no one?"

She raised her finger and waggled it in my face. "Nuh uh uh, Mr. Knighthorse. That's all on the police report."

I produced one of my business cards and placed it on the glass table. In the background on the card was a photo of the sun sinking below the blue horizon of the Pacific Ocean. The word *keen* always comes to mind. In one corner, was my smiling mug.

"Should you remember anything, please don't hesitate to call."

I set my card on the glass table; she somehow managed to not lunge for it. I finished the tea in one swallow and, leaving the way I had come, picked the mint sprig from my teeth.

Ah, dignity.

J.R. RAIN

7.

The field was wet with dew, and a low wispy mist hung over the grass. The mist made the morning look colder than it really was. Sanchez and I had been doing sprints along the width of Long Beach State's football field for the past twenty minutes. Sweat streamed down my face, and I probably had a healthy, athletic glow about me. I tried desperately to ignore the pain in my right leg. But the pain was there. Persistent, throbbing and threatening to become something more serious. But I pushed on.

"You're pretty fast," I said to Sanchez. "For a cop."

"I've got to work off the donuts."

We finished another set of sprints and were now standing around, sucking wind like we had done at UCLA years earlier, when we had both been young and not so innocent. When the world had been my oyster. Before I had shattered my leg, and before Sanchez had become an LAPD homicide detective.

There were now two female joggers circling the track around us, dressed in long black nylon jogging pants and wearing white baseball caps. They moved spryly, their identical ponytails swishing along their angular shoulder blades.

"Sooner or later we're going to have to run to the other side of the field," said Sanchez. He spoke with a slight Hispanic accent when he wasn't careful, or when he was tired. He was tired. He was watching the two joggers. "Unless you prefer to watch them all morning long."

"Worse ways of spending a morning."

"How's the leg holding up?"

I shrugged.

Sanchez grinned. "That good, huh?"

We ran back to the other side of the field, just in time to meet the two women again, who swished past us with a casual glance or two. One of them said something and the other giggled.

"They're laughing at you," said Sanchez.

"Wouldn't be the first time," I said. "By the way, I beat you this time. Bum leg and all. How does that make you feel?"

"Maybe I should shoot myself."

"Got a gun in my gym bag."

"So do I."

We raced back and as far as I could tell we were dead even this time, pulling up just past the far sidelines. The throb in my leg was feeling unhealthy. We had done this for the past thirty minutes.

"We're even on that last run," said Sanchez. "So I say we call it a morning. Baby steps. This is your first day back in training. Want to take it easy on the leg, especially a man your age."

"You're only a month younger."

"Lot can happen in a month."

"True."

We sat on a bench wet with dew. The mist was all pervasive, leaving nothing untouched. I enjoyed the solitude it allowed.

"You going back with me to San Diego?" I asked. "To try out?"

He laughed, and kept his dark eyes on the joggers. "I wasn't the one they asked to come out of retirement."

"You could make it."

"I was good, but not that good," he said. The mist was dispersing and more light was getting through. There were also more joggers now, three males, but these were not as interesting to look at.

Sanchez checked his watch. "Most people with respectable jobs have to get going now."

"Luckily, neither of us have respectable jobs."

"True," said Sanchez. "So who do you think did this girl?"

"Don't know," I said. "That's the part I'm working on."

"Isn't it just your job to get the kid off? And to give a damn who really killed the girl?"

"But I do give a damn who killed her."

"You always do. But you shouldn't. It's not your job, at least not on this case. Your job is to spring the kid before he goes to trial."

I said nothing.

"I know," said Sanchez, "I know. You'll do it your way."

I smiled brightly. "Exactly."

8.

I was sitting outside Huntington High in my car, on a stretch of road that overlooked the Pacific Ocean. My windows were down and the engine was off; a cool breeze wafted through the car. Life was good at the Beach.

It was three o'clock and school was just getting out. High schoolers nowadays are younger and smaller than I remember, although the occasional curvy creature sashayed by. Most of the girls wore unflattering jeans that rode low on the hip, showed a lot of tanned flesh and a surprising amount of lower back tattoos. The high school boys were spiked, pierced and dyed. Those who weren't natural blonds, wanted to be. Huntington High probably had a very popular surfing club. My old high school in Inglewood did not have a surfing club. We had metal detectors and hired security that were referred to as The Staff.

More than one Mercedes whipped out of the student parking lot, followed by nineteen different Mustangs, and twenty-two of the new Volkswagen bugs. I saw exactly seventeen near-fatal car accidents in the span of forty-five seconds.

The less fortunate, and those not of driving age, waited in line and boarded the various yellow school buses. Other students walked, some passing my Cobra. I was promptly ignored, being an Old Man, and Not Very Interesting.

I didn't blame them, although my ego was crushed a little.

All in all, I saw a fair share of Asians and Hispanics, but no blacks.

Teachers on duty did their best to clear out the lingering students from the front halls. The buses pulled away. And the potential smash-up derby that was the student parking lot cleared away shockingly fast and without a single incident. I waited another ten minutes, then left my car there on the hill, and headed up to the administration building at the front of the school.

The building, and much of the school, was old cinder block, bright with a fresh coat of powder blue. A very school-like color. I stepped into the mostly empty admin office. There was a receptionist behind her desk, pen in hand and working furiously. She was young and pretty, probably a school senior. I stepped up to the front desk.

"Hello," I said.

She jumped. She had been writing a personal letter, probably when she should have been working. Should I be tempted to read her musings, she quickly covered the letter with her folded hands. But not well enough. I saw the words: *asshole*, *love* and *booty* used repeatedly. Further proof that there's nothing so sweet in life as love's young dream.

When she had recovered enough to speak, she said, "Can I help you?"

I smiled engagingly and showed her my investigator license.

A hell of a picture.

"Doesn't look like you."

"It's me, I swear." I struck a similar pose, turning my head a little to the side, and blasted her with the same full wattage smile. "See?"

She shrugged. "The guy in the picture is cuter."

I wasn't sure if I should be offended. After all, it was *me* in the picture, and she was calling *that* guy cute.

"So you're a private investigator?"

"Yep."

She nodded, but her interest was already waning.

"I give autographs, too," I said.

"I don't want your autograph."

"Of course not. Who would I see about gaining permission to access your school?"

"You need to speak with Mrs. Williams."

"Great."

"Let me see if she's in."

"That would be fantastic."

"Are you always this cheery?"

"Yes!"

"Hold on."

"Super!"

She removed herself from her post, snatched up her letter, and stepped down the hall and peeked into one of the open doors. I sat down in one of the plastic chairs lining the wall and made it a point to look cheery as hell. The office was covered with senior year group photographs, dating back to the forties. The photos were lined end to end and circled the room above the windows.

"Mrs. Williams will see you now, Mr. Knighthorse."

"Keen."

"Keen?"

"I was running out of superlatives."

9.

The brass nameplate on Mrs. Williams's desk designated her as vice principal in charge of discipline. Ah, she would be the one the students hated and likened to Hitler, as all students did in all high schools to any vice principal in charge of discipline.

One difference.

She couldn't have been prettier.

Mrs. Williams stood from behind her desk and shook my hand vigorously. She gestured for me to sit and I did. She was young, perhaps the same age as me. Her hair hung loose around her shoulders and I had the impression she had recently set it free from a tight bun. Of course, the three bobby pins sitting next to her computer mouse were a dead giveaway.

I am, of course, a detective.

Mrs. Williams wore a white blouse with a wide collar that fanned across her collar bones. Her face was thin and pleasantly narrow. Of course, the intelligence behind her emerald eyes were the dead giveaway that she was something more than just a pretty face. A lot more. The eyes were arresting and disarming, true. But, good Christ, they were penetratingly cold. Chips of ice. She leveled them at me now and I squirmed in my seat.

"You seem a bit preoccupied, Mr. Knighthorse," said Mrs. Williams. "You must have a lot on your mind."

Her voice was a little husky, and a lot of sexy. The chest beneath her blouse seemed full, and heaved slightly with each breath.

"I was just wishing I had had you as my vice principal in high school."

She did not blush, and her gaze did not flick away from mine. "What are you implying?"

"You are a looker, Mrs. Williams."

She cracked a smile, and placed one hand carefully on top of the other. I could see her wedding band clearly. A plain gold band.

"A looker?"

"Means I think you're swell."

"Lord. Is this some sort of come-on line?"

"You're married, and I'm happily dating the love of my life. I am simply warming you up to get what I need."

"At least you're honest about your intentions."

"That, and I think you're a looker."

"What do you need, Knighthorse?"

"What happened to the *mister*?"

"Anyone who calls me a looker loses that formal courtesy."

"Is that a fancy way of saying I'm warming up to you?"

"Yes."

"Good. Because I need access to your school."

"What sort of access?"

Behind her the blinds were open, and I had a shot of an open quad. From here, Mrs. Williams could see much of the school. It was a good view for the vice principal of discipline to have.

"I'm here to investigate the murder of Amanda Peterson," I said. Her eyes did not waver. I forged on. "To do so I will need to speak to witnesses."

"There are no witnesses to Amanda's murder

here."

"But there are those here who could provide me some assistance, including yourself."

She leaned forward and looked down at her ring. Her smooth face had the beginnings of crow's feet. She used her thumb to toy with the ring, spinning it around her narrow finger. I wondered if perhaps she was regretting the ring was on, and thus losing an opportunity to be with yours truly. Or perhaps not.

"I'll give you access, but not during school hours, and no speaking with students."

"Agreed."

"Now what do you need from me?"

"Was Derrick the only African-American in school?"

"No. There are three others. The papers were incorrect."

"Was he a good student?"

"Exceptional. He carried a 4.0 GPA. Was on his way to USC for a full football scholarship. The world was his oyster."

"Well, I certainly wouldn't call USC an oyster, Mrs. Williams. Maybe a parasitic tiger mussel that's currently infesting the Great Lakes."

"Nice imagery. UCLA fan?"

"And their best fullback."

She raised an eyebrow. "Yes, I can see that.

You are a big boy."

"Was Derrick capable of killing?" I asked.

She spread her hands flat on the desk and smiled at me. "Derrick was strong and excelled at a violent sport. Physically he could have done it. If you are inquiring about his psyche, you are barking up the wrong tree. Derrick and I rarely crossed paths. He kept his nose clean, as my father would say."

"And being in charge of discipline, you would know."

"I would."

"Can you tell me anything about Amanda?"

"She was more trouble. But petty stuff, really. Nothing serious."

"Like what?"

"Skipping class, smoking on school grounds."

"She and Derrick an item?"

"Yes. The whole school knew that. He was our star athlete."

"And black in a nearly all-white school. Did he ever have any problems with racism?"

"As far as I knew, he was wildly popular among his fellow class mates."

"Amanda was in the school band?"

She paused, then shrugged. "I do not know. Maybe."

"I was told she quit. Any reason why?"

"Refer to my prior comment."

I didn't like the answer. Mrs. Williams probably had access to Amanda's file, and certainly would have read it since the murder. Band membership would have been in the official records.

"And Knighthorse," she said, "I am definitely not the kind of principal you wish you had in high school. Students are never, *ever* pleased to be sitting where you are now."

I smiled. "I'm not a student. And it's not a bad view from here, Mrs. Williams."

Most women would have blushed. She did not.

I left her office.

10.

The campus was sprawling and clean.

The hallways were lined with yellow lockers. Most sported combination locks, although a few were padded with locks of considerable fortitude. These were blocks of titanium padlock perfection that were engineered to protect far more important things than school books and pencils.

My footsteps echoed along the now-empty hallway. Just a half hour earlier it had been filled to overflowing with students. Within these hallowed lockered halls, plans for parties had been made, drug deals had gone down, students had been harassed, asses pinched and thoughts of teenage suicide pondered.

In the police report, Derrick claimed to have been working out at the school gym at the time of the murder. He had no alibi. His football coach often left him alone with the keys, trusting Derrick. It was against school rules, but Derrick had proven himself to be reliable, and after all he was the star athlete. The coach probably loved him like a son.

The coach was the last to see Derrick. That had been at 5:45 p.m. on the evening of the murder. The coroner's report placed the time of murder at 7:00 p.m. According to the arrest report, the detectives figured Derrick left the school weight room shortly after the coach had left and proceeded to ambush the girlfriend he loved and slaughtered her in front of her home. His vehicle had no trace of her blood. There were no wounds on Derrick's hands or arms. Other than the murder weapon found in his backseat there was nothing to link him to the murder.

The murder weapon was enough.

Had he not blundered and forgotten about the murder weapon, Derrick would have pulled off one amazingly clean murder. I've now had a chance to see the crime scene photos. The murder was definitely *not* clean.

Derrick, of course, claimed he was at the school weight room until 7:30 p.m. that night, like he was every night. A routine that anyone could have caught onto and used against him.

No one believed Derrick's story. Except his defense attorney Charlie Brown, although he was being paid handsomely to believe his story.

And me. But I was not being handsomely paid. I hate it when that happens.

I moved beyond the hallway, beyond the brick walled central quad, beyond what was probably the school cafeteria, beyond the gym, and toward the athletic department.

It was spring, and so there was no football to be practiced, which was why Derrick had been lifting weights after school, rather than working out with his team. Instead, it was baseball and track season. Beyond a chain-linked fence I could see a varsity baseball game getting under way. Parents and some students filled the small bleachers. To the north of the baseball field was a track field, and it was a beehive of activity. I watched a young girl sprint for about thirty yards and leap through the air, landing gracelessly in a cloud of dirt. She dusted herself off, and then headed back for another leap.

I followed a paved pathway, bigger than a

sidewalk, but not big enough to be called a road. The pathway skirted the softball field and headed toward a group of buildings lined with doors. One of the doors was open, and inside I could see shining new gym equipment.

My old high school did not have shining new gym equipment. It had well-used and badly damaged gym equipment. In fact, we just had free weights and a few squat racks, come to think of it.

But it had been enough, if used correctly and religiously. Both of which I had done.

I stepped into the doorway and peaked in, almost expecting to see a membership desk. What a spread. Gleaming chrome equipment covered the entire room. Mirrors were every-where. Techno rock pumped through loud speakers situated in every corner. Boys and a handful of girls were in there, all taking their workouts very seriously. I was completely ignored. In fact, there seemed to be a melan-choly mood to the place, despite the rhythmic pounding of the dance music.

I spied some offices in the back and headed that way, passing two kids lifting an impressive amount on the bench. I calculated the weight. They were benching almost three hundred pounds.

Not bad for a kid.

I came to the first office and knew I had hit the jackpot. The sign on the closed door said *Coach*.

Only the egocentricity of a football coach, in an entire department of other coaches, went by *Coach* alone.

I knocked on the closed door. Doing so, the door creaked open, and immediately I sensed something wrong. Very wrong.

Coach was a big man, and from what I could tell he had taken a bullet to the side of the head. Blood and brain matter sprayed the east side of his office. A revolver was still in his hands. The blood had not congealed, and was dripping steadily from the wound in his open head. His eyes were wide with the shock and horror of what he had done to himself.

Music thumped loudly into the office.

No one had even heard the shot.

11.

Sanchez and I were working out at a 24-Hour Fitness in Huntington Beach. It was midday, and the gym was quiet. I had worked up a hell of a sweat, and was dripping all over the place. Sanchez didn't sweat; at least not like a real man. And I let him know it again.

"I save the sweating for the bedroom," he said, finishing off his third and final set of military presses. "Women like that."

"You married your high school sweetheart. You don't know shit about what women want."

"Fine," he said, wiping down the machine. "Danielle likes it when I sweat. Shows her I take my lovemaking seriously. Besides, Danielle is a lot of woman."

"Yes," I said, "she is."

We moved over to the incline presses. Together we added weight until we ran out of plates.

"Place is going to hell," said Sanchez, looking around, then swiping two forty-fives from another bench.

"Yes, but it's cheap. And apparently open twenty-four hours."

"You sound like a goddamn commercial." He handed me one of the plates and we pushed each into place. The bar looked very unstable and heavily overloaded. "We're attracting attention again."

I had eased down onto the incline bench. In the mirror I could see that two or three young guys, including some gym trainers, were now watching us. I ignored them. So did Sanchez, who spotted me by standing on a steel platform. The forty-five pound bar was sagging. Weight clanked as I went through my twelve reps. I focused on the Chargers training camp, which was coming up soon. This motivated me, pushed me to lift more and work harder. I focused on looking good for Cindy. This motivated me as well. Only on the last rep did

Sanchez lend some help. Then he guided the barbell into place.

"Didn't need your help on the twelfth," I said.

"Sure you didn't," he said.

A voice said: "Hey, man, how much weight is that?"

We both turned. He was a surfer. Bleached hair and some minor muscle tone. He had a piercing in his nose, and some idiotic Chinese pictographs up and down his arm.

"You too stupid to do the math?" asked Sanchez. He turned to me. "Kids nowadays."

"Kids nowadays," I added sagely.

The surfer looked at the weight we were hefting and decided that he would not take offense. He left. Good decision.

Sanchez did his twelve reps, and to be a dick I helped him with the last two. After two more sets each, we sat down on opposing benches and sipped from our water bottles.

"He leave a suicide note?" asked Sanchez.

"Nothing," I said. "But he had been fired earlier that day."

"Why?"

I shrugged. "He'd been taking a lot of shit about leaving Derrick alone on the night of the murder."

"Hell of a thing to be fired over."

"Uh huh."

"Papers say he was a hell of a coach," said Sanchez.

"Three CIF championships."

"Why do you think he popped himself?"

"Hard to say," I said. "Detective Hanson tells me the man was divorced earlier in the year. They say divorced men are the highest risk for suicide."

"Thank you for that useless bit of fucking trivia."

I ignored him, and continued.

"Add to that your best athlete being accused of a heinous murder, and compound it with losing your job...."

I shrugged again.

"You shrug a lot for a detective," said Sanchez.

"I know. It's part of the job description."

We moved over to the squat rack. We slammed on as many forty-fives as we could find, then some thirty-fives.

"You know," said Sanchez, "people here think we're freaks. Maybe we should go to a real gym."

"I like it here," I said, hunkering down under the bar and placing my feet exactly the width of my shoulders. "Besides, it's open twenty-four hours."

Sanchez shook his head.

12.

He was watching me knowingly with those nondescript eyes. Nondescript only in color, that is. Everything else about them was, well, very *non*-nondescript.

He knows what you're thinking.

The words flashed across my mind, along with the popular Christmas tune, and a chill went through me.

I was having another Big Mac. Or three. He was drinking another coffee. Lukewarm and black. Just like I like my women. Kidding.

"So have you told anyone about me?" he asked.

"That I speak to God in a McDonald's?"

"Yes."

"Everyone I know. Hell, even people I don't know. In fact, I just told the sixteen-year-old gal working behind the counter that I was meeting with God in a few minutes and could she hurry."

"And what did she say?"

"Said she was going to call the cops."

Jack shook his head and sipped some more of his coffee. I noticed he still had the same streaks of dirt along his forehead.

"So your answer is no," he said.

"Of course it's no, and if you were God you would know that."

He said nothing; I said nothing. A very old man had sat in a booth next to us. The old man smiled at Jack, and Jack smiled back. The man leaned over and spoke to us.

"I'm coming home soon," he said.

"Yes," said Jack. "You are."

"I'm ready," said the old man, and sat back in his seat and proceeded to consume a gooey cinnamon roll.

"What was that about?" I asked Jack, not bothering to lower my voice. Hell, the man was as old as the hills, no way he could overhear us.

"He's going to die tonight," said Jack, rather nonchalantly, I thought.

"Well," I said after a moment, "his heart could only take so many cinnamon rolls."

Jack looked at me and sipped his coffee carefully, cradling the paper cup in both hands. He said nothing.

"Why do you drink with both hands?" I finally asked.

"I enjoy the feel of the warm cup."

"And why do you look at me so closely?"

"I enjoy soaking in the details of a moment."

We had gone over this before.

"Live in the moment," I repeated. "And all that other bullshit."

"Yes," he said. "And all that other bullshit."

"There is no past and there is no future," I continued, on a holy roll.

"Exactly."

"Only the moment," I said.

"You're getting it, Jim. Good."

"No, I'm not, actually. You see, Jack, I know for a fact that there is a past because a young girl got slaughtered outside her house. In the past."

"You have taken a personal interest in the case, I see."

"And now someone has killed themselves. A coach at the same high school—but, of course, you know all of this."

Jack sat unmovingly, watching me closely.

"I saw his brains on the wall and I saw the hole in his head," I continued. "Damn straight this case has gotten personal."

We were silent. I could hear myself breathing, my breath running ragged in my throat. I had gotten worked up.

"You know, it's damn hard having a conversation with someone who claims to know everything," I said, concluding.

"I never claimed to know everything. You assume I know everything."

"Well, do you?"

"Yes."

"Well, fuck me. There you go."

"But you're forgetting something," said Jack patiently. He was always patient, whoever the hell he was.

"No," I said. "Don't tell me."

"Yes," he said, telling me anyway. "You, too, know everything."

We had gone over this before, dozens of times.

"The answers are always within you," he said.

"Would have been nice to know during algebra tests."

"You knew the answers then, just as you

know them now."

"Bullshit."

He smiled serenely.

"If you say so," he said.

"Fine," I said, "So how is it that I know everything, when, in fact, I don't feel like I know shit?"

"First of all, you know everything because you are a part of me," he said.

"Part of a bum?"

"Sure," he said. "We are all one. You, me and everyone you see."

"So I know the answers because you know the answers," I said.

"Something like that," he said. "Mostly, you know the answers because the answers have already been revealed to you. Would you like an example?"

"Please."

"What's the Atomic symbol for gold?"

"Wait, I know this one." I rubbed my head. "Fuck. I don't remember. Wait, I'll take a stab at it: *G-O*?"

"No, it's *A-U*."

"At least I was close."

"What's the Atomic symbol for gold?" he asked again.

"*A-U*," I said without thinking. "Wait, I only know that because you just told me."

"Yeah, so?"

"Well, I didn't know a few seconds ago."

"Are you living now, or are you living a few seconds ago?"

"I'm living now, of course, but if I didn't have you here to give me the answer—and by the way, I'm not convinced *A-U* is the right answer—I still wouldn't know the answer."

"Shall we try another example?" he asked.

"Yes," I said, "but this time don't give me the freakin' answer."

"What's the Atomic symbol for Mercury?"

"No idea," I said.

"None?"

"Nope. *M-E*?"

"No."

"See, told you I didn't know the answer."

"You were right," he said. "And I was wrong, apparently."

"Fuck. I'm going to go look it up tonight on the internet, aren't I?"

He shrugged.

"And then when I do, I'll have the answer."

He took a sip from his coffee.

"But I still don't have the answer now, but I will soon," I said.

He yawned a little.

"And since time doesn't exist, that means I always had the answer."

He shrugged again and drank the rest of his coffee.

"I'm still not buying any of this shit," I said.

13.

According to homicide investigators, Amanda Peterson had been returning home from a high school party on the night of her murder.

Returning home at 7:30 p.m.

Isn't that about the time most parties get started? Perhaps she was going home to fetch something she had forgotten. Perhaps not. Either way, I sniffed a clue here.

Thanks to Mrs. Williams, vice principal extraordinaire, I now had a small list of Amanda

Peterson's known friends from high school. To help facilitate my investigation, Mrs. Williams gave me the home addresses to the three names on the list. I thought that was a hell of a nice gesture on her part, and reminded myself to repay her with one of my most winning smiles.

The first house on the list was a massive colonial with a pitched roof, numerous gables and a wide portico. I pulled into the wrap-around driveway.

The doorbell was answered by a cute teenage girl wearing matching sweatshirt and sweatpants that said UCLA. A girl after my own heart. She was blond, pretty, and quite small, no more than five foot two. Her big blue eyes were filled with intelligence.

"Can I speak with Rebecca Garner?" I asked.

"You got her."

"My name's Jim Knighthorse and I'm a private investigator."

She smiled broadly, and her eyes widened with pleasure. I turned around to see who the hell she was smiling at. Turns out it was me.

"A real private investigator," she said, clapping.

"In the flesh."

She turned somber on a dime. "You're here about Amanda."

"Yes."

"Mrs. Williams called and asked if it was okay to give out our address. So I knew you'd be coming by."

"Are your parents home?"

"No, I'm alone, so maybe we should talk out here." She stepped through the doorway and shut the door behind her. "My parents said it would be okay for me to talk to you."

She led me to a wooden rocking bench facing the street. Rebecca, utilizing the full use of the bench, rocked us back and forth. A minute later, I was feeling seasick. I stopped the rocking.

"Sorry," she said. "I'm just a little nervous. I've never talked to a real live detective before."

"Well, you're doing a great job of it so far." I pointed at the UCLA logo. "Obviously you're highly intelligent and wise for your age if you intend to go there."

She looked down. "My dad went there."

"He must be highly intelligent and wise himself."

"He's a doctor. Intelligent, but I don't know about wise. Anyway, he's never home, so I really wouldn't know."

"How old are you?"

"Seventeen."

"You're a junior?"

"Yes."

We were silent. She started rocking again, and I put my foot out to stop it again. She ducked her head and said, "Oops."

"Were you with Amanda on the last day she was alive?"

"Yes."

"Tell me about the party."

"We got there around seven. Amanda and I went together because Derrick was working out at the gym, as usual. He's so boring. He never likes to party. All he ever did was work out, play sports and hang out with Amanda."

"Did he love Amanda?"

She shifted her weight. The bench creaked slightly. I kept my foot firmly planted. No more swinging today. Rebecca looked away, brushing aside a blond strand that had stuck to her shiny lip gloss.

"Oh, yeah. He loved her a lot."

"You think he killed her?"

"No."

"You say that pretty quick."

"He loved her so much. He would have done anything for her."

"Was Amanda seeing someone else?"

"No. But at the time, there was another guy who wouldn't leave her alone."

"Who?"

"Chris, the guy who threw the party. He's always liked her."

"Did she fool around with Chris?"

"No. She never cheated on Derrick. They really did love each other. It was sweet watching the two of them together. They were always together and holding each other and kissing."

"Tell me about Chris."

"He's a senior. Used to play football, but got kicked off the team because he's an asshole. You like football?"

"Yes," I said.

"I don't understand it. Just a bunch of boys jumping on each other."

"That about sums it up."

"They kicked him off the team because he was a partier and did drugs and probably never showed up for practice."

"That'll do it."

"He always had it pretty bad for Amanda. I mean, you've seen her picture. She is—was—so pretty. A lot of guys at school liked her."

"Especially Chris."

"Especially Chris. He hated Derrick. Hated him."

"Why?"

She looked at me as if I were the beach idiot. "Because Derrick had his girl, and because Derrick was black. He was always making comments to Amanda."

"Racially insensitive comments?" I offered.

"Yes," she said. "Those kinds of comments. Everywhere she went, he let her know it. It was horrible."

"Then why go to Chris's party?"

She shrugged. "It's high school, it was the only party being thrown that night. Plus Amanda said that Chris personally invited her and had apologized for being such a jerk."

"So what happened at the party?"

"Chris was drunk when we got there. He was being a real dick. Usual Chris, you know."

"Oh, I know."

"You know him?"

"No, I'm just being supportive."

She smiled and shook her head. "You're kind of funny."

"Kind of."

"So anyway, we get to the party and almost immediately Chris hits on Amanda. You know, puts his arm around her and tries to kiss her, just being an asshole."

"What did Amanda do?"

"She pushed him away."

"How did Chris react?"

"Same old shit. Put her down, put Derrick down." She grinned. "Derrick's already kicked Chris's ass once for giving Amanda a hard time."

"Sounds like Chris needs another ass kicking."

"Hard to do that from jail."

I nodded. "So what happened next?"

"Amanda was pretty upset and left the party. I offered to go with her, but she refused, saying she wanted to be alone."

I didn't add that if Rebecca had been with Amanda, that Amanda stood a better chance of being alive today. Then again, there might be two dead teenage girls instead of one.

"That was the last time you saw her?"

She was looking away, blinking hard. "Yes."

"After Amanda left, what did Chris do?"

"I don't know. He took off in his car."

Oh?

"Did you tell the police this?" I asked.

"The police never came by."

"The police assume Derrick did the killing," I said.

"I don't blame them," she said. "But I think someone set Derrick up."

"I do too."

"Someone who doesn't like him very much," she said.

"I agree. Where does Chris live?"

She told me, and I gave her my card.

"Nice picture," she said.

"Like I said, you are obviously a bright and intelligent young lady."

I left her rocking alone on the bench swing.

14.

According to Rebecca, Chris's house was three streets down. Look for the broken garage door and red mailbox. Turns out the house was seven streets down. She was close. Okay, not really.

There was no one home, so I waited in my car, which really was my home away from home. I had wasted more time sitting in it than I care to dwell on. One of these days I was going to wise up and keep an emergency novel in the glove box for just such an occasion. I turned on the radio and listened to various sports radio programs. There had once been a time when I was the subject of sports radio. At least locally. Maybe again someday. I looked at my watch. An hour of my life had passed. I turned off the radio and put my seat back. The police hadn't investigated Amanda's murder very thoroughly. That much was obvious. They were confident the killer was Derrick. They had no reason to believe otherwise, and they did not look for a reason. Looking for a reason made their job harder than it had to be, especially when a kid with a knife was looking them straight in the face. According to the homicide report, an anonymous caller had tipped the police that the knife was in the backseat of Derrick's car. Convenient.

Two hours later, after a fitful nap, a silver Corvette squealed around the corner and bounded into the driveway. A lanky kid hopped out and stared at me.

More than ready for a little action, I leapt out of my car and, perhaps a little too eagerly, approached him. The kid backed up a step.

"Chris Randall?" I asked.

He was about an inch shorter than me, about half the width of me, and certainly not as good looking. Not everyone can be me.

"Who are you?" he asked.

I told him.

"You have a badge or something?" he asked. There was mild humor in his voice, and a whole lot of cockiness. I've been told the same.

"Or something." I showed him my investigator's license. "Can I talk to you about Amanda Peterson?"

His shoulders bunched at the mention of her name. He recovered and walked around to the Vette's trunk and popped it open with the push of a button on his keychain. He reached inside and pulled out a ratty backpack. His hands were shaking. When he spoke again, the humor was gone from his voice, although there was still an underlying tone of arrogance. My question had unsettled him. "Sure. Go ahead."

"She was last seen leaving your party."

He slung the pack over a bony shoulder. "Probably should have stayed, huh?"

"Probably. You were also seen leaving the party shortly thereafter."

"Yeah, so."

I smiled broadly, just your friendly neighborhood detective. "So where'd you go?"

"Why should I tell you?"

"Have you talked to the police yet?"

"No."

"Then they would be interested to know that prior to Amanda leaving the party that you had verbally abused her and made racially insensitive remarks about her boyfriend Derrick."

He looked at me some more, then shrugged. "I went on a beer run."

"Where?"

"Corner of Eighth and Turner." He leaned a hip against the Vette's fender. The mild amusement was back. His eyes almost twinkled. "You think I killed her?"

I shrugged. "Just doing my job."

"They found the knife in Derrick's car."

"Knives can be planted," I said.

"Why would I kill her?"

"You tell me."

"I wouldn't," he said. "I liked her a lot."

"Maybe you were jealous."

"Of the nigger?"

"Of the African-American. Yes. He had Amanda, and you didn't."

"Then why not kill him? Doesn't make sense."

"No," I said. "Sometimes it doesn't."

"Well, fuck you." He turned and headed up to his front door.

"Have a good day," I said. "Study hard."

Without turning, he flipped me the bird.

Kids these days. They grow up so fast.

15.

Sanchez and I were in the backroom of the Kwik Mart on Eighth and Turner.

We had convinced the reluctant owner, a small Vietnamese man named Phan, to allow us to review his security tapes on the night of Amanda's murder. We informed him that he had sold alcohol to a minor, and that we could prove it, but in exchange for his cooperation, he would receive only a warning. He obliged.

When Phan was done setting up the VCR, he handed me the remote control. The store owner left us alone, mumbling under his breath.

"You speak Vietnamese?" asked Sanchez.

"Nope."

"What's the chances he's praising us for our diligent investigative work?"

"Slim to none."

We both leaned back in a worn leather love seat, the only seating available in the back room.

"Just because we're in a love seat," said Sanchez, "doesn't mean I love you."

"Sure you do," I said. "You just don't know it yet."

I had the remote control and was fast forwarding through the day of her murder. In the bottom right corner was the time.

At seven thirty I let the tape play in real time. Sanchez put his hands behind his head and stretched.

"Should have brought some popcorn," he said.

"They have some in the store. I think Phuong might be inclined to give us some on the house."

"His name was Phan, and that would be abuse of power. We would be on the take."

"For some popcorn, it would be worth it."

"But only if buttered."

We watched the comings and goings of

many different people of many different nationalities, most of them buying cigarettes and Lotto tickets, all slapping their money down on the counter. The camera angled down from over the clerk's shoulder, giving us a clear shot of each customer's face.

"Oh, she's cute," said Sanchez.

"The brunette?"

"No, the blond."

"What is it with you and brunettes, anyway?" he asked.

"Brunettes are beautiful. Blonds are pretty. There's a difference."

"You're blond."

"There always an exception to every rule."

At seven thirty-eight a young man approached the counter carrying two cases of Miller Genuine Draft. Tall and lanky. The owner studied him carefully, then shrugged, and took the kid's money.

"That our boy?" asked Sanchez.

"Yes."

"The time of death was seven thirty?"

"Yes," I said.

"Kid can't be in two places at once."

"No," I said.

"The kid didn't do her."

"No, he didn't."

I stopped the tape and we sat back on the

sofa.

"Which means someone was waiting for her at her house," I said. "So how did this someone know Amanda would be leaving the party early?"

We were silent. Two great investigative minds at work.

"Don't know," said Sanchez.

"Me neither," I said.

"Maybe she was followed home."

"Or just a random killing."

Sanchez looked at me and grinned. "Seems like you've got your work cut out for you, kiddo."

16.

It was a late April morning in Huntington Beach, California, which meant, of course, that the weather was perfect.

Why the hell would anyone want to live anywhere else?

I was sitting at my desk, reviewing a sampling of the San Diego Chargers playbook, a sampling that Rob, Cindy's brother, had just faxed to me. Rob let it be known that this was Highly Classified material, and that his job was on the line. I reminded him that I was boffing his sister, and that practically made me family. He told me that he never wanted to hear the words *boffing* and *his sister* in the same sentence again and that he was going to get drunk at our wedding and make a nuisance of himself. I told him there would be no wedding because his sister wasn't marriage material. He told me to fuck off, and hung up.

The plays were complex, but not rocket science. The majority faxed to me involved the fullback position, which was my position. I studied them with interest, making my own notes along the borders.

And that's when the guy with the gun showed up.

***

I heard the door open, and when I looked up the Browning 9mm was pointed at my head. I hate when that happens.

"Can I help you?" I asked.

"Shut the hell up, fuck nut."

"Fuck nut. The one nut Home Depot doesn't carry."

The man was probably in his fifties, gray hair sleeked back with a lot of gel. He wore a gold hoop in his left ear, pirate-like. Indeed, in his misspent youth he probably always wanted to be a pirate or a buccaneer, only I didn't really know the difference between the two. Had it been fashionable, he would have worn a patch over his eye. His face, all in all, was hideous, heavily pock-marked, sunken and sallow. The gun never wavered from my face.

"What's the difference between a pirate and a buccaneer?" I asked.

"Shut the fuck up."

"I don't know either. Nothing to be ashamed of."

His eyes, for all intents and purposes, were dead. Lifeless. Lacking sympathy, compassion, or caring. The eyes of a killer, rapist, suicidal bomber, genocidal dictator. His eyes made me nervous, to say the least. Eyes like that were capable of anything. Anything. They kill your family, your babies, your children, your husbands and wives. I only knew one other man who had eyes like that, and he was my father.

The Browning never wavered from my face. "You're working on a case," the man said.

"I'm working on a few cases. It's what I do. See that filing cabinet behind me, it's full of pending cases. The shelf on the bottom is full of my closed cases."

There was a heavy silence.

"You're going to call me a *fuck nut* again aren't you?" I said. "It feels like a *fuck nut* moment, doesn't it?"

He pulled the trigger. My ear exploded with pain. I tried not to flinch, although I might have, dammit. If he had chosen that moment to call me a *fuck nut* I might have missed it...due to the excessive ringing in my head.

The bullet had punctured a picture frame behind me. I heard the glass tinkling down. I did not know yet which picture it had been, although it would have been one of the featured articles about yours truly.

That's when I felt something drip onto my shoulder. I touched my ear. Blood. The bullet grazed my lobe.

"You shot me," I said.

"We want you off the Derrick Booker case," he said. "Or the next shot won't miss."

"But you didn't miss. You shot my earlobe. Get it straight."

"I heard you would be a smart ass."

"Sometimes I am a smart ass. Now I'm just pissed. You shot me."

"We meet again and I kill you."

"You shot me," I said. "We meet again and I owe you one."

He grinned and proceeded to shoot out five or six framed pictures behind me. I didn't move. The cacophony of tinkling glass and resounding gunshots filled my head and office.

He pointed the gun at my forehead and said, "Bang, fuck nut."

He backed out of my office and shut the door.

And I went back to my playbook. My ears were ringing and my earlobe stung.

The fuck nut.

17.

On the way home from the office I stopped by the local liquor store and bought a bottle of Scotch and some Oreos. The Scotch was for getting drunk, and the Oreos were for gaining weight. At two-hundred and ten pounds I was still too small for an NFL fullback.

Cindy was away tonight at UC Santa Barbara's School of Anthropology giving a guest lecture on what it means to be human.

Hell, he thought, I could have saved everyone a trip out to Santa Barbara. Being human meant walking into any liquor store from here to Nantucket and buying a bottle of Scotch and a bag of Oreos. Let's see the chimps pull that one off.

Cindy Darwin was a favorite on the guest lecture circuit. Any anthropology department worth their salt wanted Cindy Darwin's ruminations on the subject of evolution. Really, she was their messiah, their prophet and savior.

She had wanted me to come with her up the coast, but I had declined, stating there were some leads I needed to follow.

Which was bullshit, really. True I had made a few phone calls prior to leaving the office, but I could have done those on my cell. I wasn't proud that I had fibbed to the love of my life. The only lead I needed to follow was my nose to the scotch and Oreos.

Cindy did not know the extent of my drinking. And if it meant fibbing to keep it that way, then fine. I drank alone and in my apartment. I harmed no one but myself and my liver.

I lived in a five story yellow stucco apartment building that sat on the edge of the Pacific Coast Highway, and overlooked Huntington State Beach. I parked in my allotted spot, narrowly missing the wooden pole that separated my spot from the car next to mine. And for training purposes only, I hauled my ass up five flights of stairs. The bag of Oreos and the bottle of scotch were heavy on my mind.

Those, and the prick who took a pot shot at my earlobe.

Inside my apartment, surrounded by shelves of paperback thrillers and my own rudimentary artwork, I tossed my keys and wallet next to the stove, grabbed my secret stash of cigarettes and pulled up a chair on my balcony.

I had a wonderful view. And should probably be paying a lot more for this apartment, but the landlord was a Bruin fan and he appreciated my efforts to beat SC through the years. So he gave me a hell of a deal, and in return he often showed up at my apartment to drink and relive the glory days. I didn't mind reliving the glory days. The glory days were all I had.

Now I hoped to make new glory days with the Chargers.

We'll see.

I opened the bag of Oreos and commenced my training, bulking up with one Oreo after another. I washed them down with swigs from the bottle of scotch, as a real man should.

When I was tired of the Oreos, after about the thirtieth, I took out a cigarette and tried like hell to give myself lung cancer.

I watched the ocean. Flat and black in the night. The lights of Catalina twinkled beyond a low haze. Further out the lights of a half dozen oil rigs blinked. And somewhere below the water was a cold world filled with life. The secret world, where sharks ate seals, where manta rays glided, where whales sang their beautiful songs.

Sometimes I wanted to jump into that cold world and never emerge, especially after the destruction of my leg.

That's when the drinking began. Few knew about my drinking. I did it alone and I did it hard, and I did it until I could drink no more. Until I could forget what was stolen from me by one fluke play by a son-of-a-bitch who chop blocked me.

My goddamn leg had been throbbing ever since Sanchez and I had been running sprints every morning for the past week. I was a step slower. I could feel it within me. Sluggish. Maybe too slow for the NFL.

And I had a goddamn kid in jail for murder one. And he was innocent. Because if he was guilty the asshole with the slicked back gray hair would not have felt it necessary to pierce my ear with a 9mm.

I had to stop drinking. I had to reclaim what was mine. And the smoking didn't help, either.

But on this night I continued to drink. And smoke. And eat the Oreos. Gluttony at its fucking worst.

The lights continued to blink on the ocean.

The night was slipping away with each swallow from the bottle and hit from the cigarette. I heard music and voices coming from Main Street below my apartment. Lots of laughter.

I didn't feel like laughing.

J.R. RAIN

18.

It was Sunday evening.

Cindy and I were at my place. We were waiting for Restaurant Express to deliver our food. I don't cook, unless you count cereal or PB&J's. The last meal I cooked, an experimental spaghetti with too much of everything from my spice rack, was promptly emptied into the garbage disposal. We considered my cooking a failure and decided that I was more useful in other areas.

We were sitting next to each other on my

leather couch in my living room, with my blinds open to my patio. We had a good view of clear skies and open water. Bob Seger crooned in the background. Our knees touched. When our knees touched I usually became excited. I was excited now, and that was nothing new. Cindy had brought her orange Pomeranian named Ginger. Ginger was likely to pee on me when she got excited. Unfortunately she got excited every time she saw me. I have learned to make it a point for her to see me first outside.

"So am I still useful in other areas?" I asked Cindy now.

"Are you harkening back to what we have come to think of as The Great Spaghetti Debacle?"

"Yes."

Cindy was dressed in jean shorts and a yellow tank top. Both showed off her naturally wonderful tan. She had a lot of Italian in her, which accounted for the coloring. Her brown hair was pulled back in a loose ponytail. Her face was smooth and without make up. She didn't need make up, anyway. But when she did...Lord help me.

"Hmm. You have your purposes," she said, sipping her glass of chardonnay.

"Is one of those purposes my usefulness in the bedroom?"

"I have uses for you in the bedroom."

"We have time before our dinner arrives."

She looked at her watch. "Should be here in ten minutes."

"Like I said, we have time."

She didn't need much more encouragement than that. With Ginger on the pergo floor below, running laps around the bed, I served one of my useful purposes.

Twice.

***

We were now on the balcony. The balcony was devoid of last night's cigarette butts and Oreo crumbs. We were sharing a glass patio table, eating cheese tortellini and drinking chardonnay.

"Does Sanchez have any idea who threatened you?" asked Cindy.

"He doesn't recognize him, but Sanchez works primarily in L.A. He's going to ask his cop buddies around here."

"Who do you think this guy works for?" she asked.

"I'm willing to bet for someone who doesn't want me to find the true killer."

"So you think the boy's innocent?"

"Now more than ever."

"What do the police think?"

"They think I'm a nuisance. Nothing new. They think this is an open and shut case and resent the fact that I'm poking around on their turf. In essence, calling them fools and liars and incompetent."

"Are you?"

"In this case, yes."

"Will you call your father?"

I felt my shoulders bunch with irritation, but let it slide. She was only trying to help.

"No."

She patted my arm, soothing me. "Of course not. You don't need him. You are your own man. I'm sorry if I offended. I just worry about you."

"I know."

We were quiet. Ginger was chasing a fly that was almost as big as her.

"The man who came to your office, he was a hired killer?"

"Yes."

"You could see it in his eyes?"

"He looked like a shark. Dead eyes."

"You sometimes get that look," said Cindy, pushing her plate away. She had eaten most of it, but had left exactly three tortellinis. I was still hopeful they would go forgotten. But the woman had a bottomless stomach, to my chagrin.

"You mean in the bedroom when my eyes roll up during the final throes of passion."

"Final throes of passion?"

"Means before I climax."

"Thank you for that clarification. No, I'm referring to the bar fight in Matzalan. I thought you were going to kill the guy. But you emerged from that look, sort of came back to your senses. I always considered that man lucky to be alive, lucky that you found yourself before you killed him."

I said nothing. I remembered that night. A barroom fight, nothing more. The man had felt up Cindy on her way to the bathroom. Bad move.

She suddenly leaned over and kissed my ear above the scab. It was a heartbreakingly sweet thing to do. She took my hand and led me into the living room, to my sofa. We sat together.

She said, "You were a devastating football player. And you may very well be again. It is a violent sport that you excel at. I would not love you if you were not always able to come back down from whatever heights you need to scale to fight and even kill."

We were silent for a few minutes.

"Almost makes you think I am at the apex of evolution," I said. "A handsome, physically imposing, intellectually stimulating, emotionally sophisticated brute."

She put her head on my shoulder.

I was on a roll. "I will even permit you to take me to your classes for show and tell, as an example of a well-evolved human being. And in contrast we can take your last boyfriend and have him stand next to me."

"Are you quite done?"

"Quite."

"Will you need protection?" she asked, wrapping her arm through mine and holding me close to her chest.

"I can take care of myself."

She patted my hand. "I know."

Ginger was jumping up and down, doing her best to leap onto the couch, but missing the mark by about a foot. I reached down and picked her up and set her in my lap. She turned three circles quickly, and then found a nook and buried her cold nose where our arms intertwined.

"How is your leg?" she asked.

"I am worried about my leg."

When I looked down at her hand, I saw that she was holding something between her thumb and forefinger. It was a black cap. The cap to my scotch. She had said nothing, simply held me, and let me know that she knew about my drinking. But she didn't say anything. Didn't have to.

I held her close. She quit playing with the cap and held it tight in her fist.

19.

I parked my car in front of the murder site. The same decayed heap of flowers still marked the place where Amanda had been found slain. There might have been a new teddy bear in the front row, but it was hard to tell. Anyway, he was a cute little guy holding a red heart balloon that said: "I Miss You."

I got out and headed up the stone pathway through the grass, passing a limestone circular fountain that was currently turned off. Leaves were collecting in the drain, and I suspected it might be a while until the fountain, with its gurgling expectations, would be turned on again.

When I reached the door, it swung open as if on its own volition.

Actually, *not* on its own volition. A cute little girl, perhaps eight, was standing in the doorway, staring up at me. She was the spitting image of Amanda.

"Is your mom or dad home?" I asked.

"You're big."

"I know."

"You're bigger than daddy."

"I'm bigger than most daddies."

"Really?"

"Uh huh."

She giggled.

A cute little black cat worked its way through the little girl's ankles. A blue bell jingled around its neck. The cat came right up to me and I scratched it between its ears. It was purring before I even touched it.

"That's Tinker Bell," said the little girl.

"He's cute."

"I love him."

"I bet you do."

"Alyssa honey, where are you?" There was a note of panic in the woman's voice.

"There's a policeman at the door, mommy."

"I'm not a policeman," I said.

The door was pulled all the way open and a woman folding a pair of briefs appeared. She was the older version of Amanda. The original version. She stared at me with eyes that were too blank, too red, too distant and too dead. She was dressed in a gray T-shirt and white shorts that revealed a fading tan.

"Mrs. Peterson?" I asked.

She paused, the white briefs hanging over her hand. "Who are you? You're not a policeman."

"I'm a private investigator," I said. "Can I speak with you? About Amanda."

She looked at me some more. A minute passed. Finally, she turned and disappeared into the darkness of her own home.

She left the door open. I took a deep breath and followed her in.

***

After asking if I would like a cup of coffee, and with my answer being in the affirmative, she promptly brought me one and set it in front of me.

I needed something to do with my hands, because Amanda's mother was making me nervous. She was in a bad place, a place I had emerged from years ago after the murder of my own mother. I knew what she was going through, but I did not want to empathize too much. I did not want to return to the bad place myself.

I was sitting in a thick sofa chair that matched the massive sofa near the fireplace, where Mrs. Peterson now sat. She reached into her black purse, which sat at her feet like an obedient dog, and removed a metal flask. She promptly poured a finger or two of something dark and bourbony into her coffee.

"More medicine, mom?" said the younger version of Amanda, who trailed in from the kitchen.

"Yes, dear. Now leave the adults alone."

She did. Sort of. She grabbed a pink Barbie backpack, plopped on the floor near the rear sliding glass door, and proceeded to remove a Barbie and Ken doll from the bag. I noted that both were nude.

"How can I help you, Mr. Knighthorse?" asked Mrs. Peterson. She was looking down at one of my nifty business cards on the coffee table before her. But before I could answer she moved on. "Are you Indian? Your name sounds Indian."

"My great grandfather was Apache. Apparently granny had a taste for savages."

"I wouldn't call them sava—oh, I see,

you're kidding."

"Yes, ma'am. But the Native American in me is diluted. Mostly, I'm German and Welch and a whole lot of man."

She looked up at me and almost smiled. "You certainly are a whole lot of man. I should have guessed the German: blond hair, tall and muscular. Would have done Hitler proud."

"I would have done anyone proud, ma'am."

"A true *knight* in shining armor."

She might have sounded flirty if her words were not empty and devoid of meaning. Like listening to a corpse speak from the grave.

"You're here to try to clear Derrick?" she said.

"Yes."

She drank from her spiked coffee. "So what the hell can I do for you?"

"First of all, I would like to express my condolences."

"How very sweet of you."

"Do you feel the police have found your daughter's killer?"

"You get right to it."

"I'm sorry if I offended."

"No. I like it. No reason to dance around the subject. My daughter was torn apart just inches from our front door by a goddamn animal."

Her voice never rose an octave. She spoke in

a monotone, although her lower lip quivered slightly.

"Mrs. Peterson, did you ever meet Derrick?" I asked.

She nodded and looked away. She was watching Alyssa play with her oddly nude dolls. "Call me Cat. For Cathy." She continued to watch Alyssa. Now Ken and Barbie were kissing in her hands. Butt naked.

"What did you think of Derrick?" I said.

"I thought he was wonderful. Charming, energetic. He seemed to really care about Amanda."

"I liked him, too," said Alyssa suddenly. Her voice echoed slightly in the darkened room. The upbeat child-like quality seemed out of place, but somehow appreciated. At least by me.

"Why did you like him?" I asked her.

"He made me laugh. Amanda loooved him."

"That's enough," said her mother quietly. Then to me: "Yes. He seemed to love her as well."

"But he was not permitted to come around?" I asked.

"No. Her father had strict rules about her dating African-Americans."

"Did you agree with the rule?"

"I wanted peace in my house."

"Did Amanda ever come to you about

Derrick?"

"Yes. Privately, quietly. We would often talk about Derrick. She had more than a crush on him. They had been dating for over a year. She might have loved him, if you want to call it that."

"Love knows no age."

She didn't say anything.

"So you didn't condone her secretly seeing Derrick?"

"No. I encouraged her."

She almost lost it right then and there. Her lip vibrated violently, but stopped when she bit down on it.

"Mrs. Peterson, you did not condemn your daughter to death by encouraging her to see Derrick."

She turned and faced me. Her eyes were full of tears. A red splotch was spreading down from her forehead. She was getting herself worked up. Before she could unleash some unholy hellfire in my direction, I quickly added, "Cat, I was threatened by an unknown killer a few days ago to stay away from this case. The killer, I assume, represents the true murderer of your daughter. It's the only thing that makes sense. I believe Derrick is innocent."

She blinked. The splotch receded. "But you are not backing off the case," she said.

"No."

"Thank you," she said. "Thank you for trying to help. I never believed in Derrick's guilt, but aren't you afraid?"

"I am a big guy. I can take care of myself."

And that's when the front door open and Mr. Peterson came in.

The first thing I noticed was that both Cat and Alyssa shrank back into themselves. Especially Alyssa. The cute little girl disappeared. Replaced by something cold and wet, and left out in the rain to die.

20.

He strode quickly into the living room, head swiveling, trying to take in everything at once. He was wearing black slacks, cordovan loafers and a black silk shirt. Sunglasses rode high on his graying head of curly hair. His roaming, pale eyes finally settled on me.

"Who the fuck are you?" he said to me.

"Richard...." said Cat, but her voice was weak, her words trailing.

I stood, "I'm Jim 'the fuck' Knighthorse."

I held out my hand. He didn't take it. Little

Alyssa was right. I was bigger than her father, had the guy by about two inches. It was clear that he lifted weights: thick chest and small waist. But he lifted for show. I know the type.

"What the fuck are you doing here?" he asked.

Richard Peterson turned to his wife, who flinched unconsciously. Or perhaps consciously. Maybe he *preferred* the women in his life to flinch in his presence. He next turned to his daughter. She was looking down, pressed against the glass of the sliding door.

I said I was here to investigate the murder of his daughter.

"Who hired you?"

I told him.

"Get out," he said. "Get the fuck out."

I didn't move at first. He then turned and looked at the little girl.

"Go to your room," he said. "Now."

Alyssa jumped and ran away, leaving her Barbie's where they lay, with Ken on top of Barbie. I saw that there was a small puddle of urine where she had been sitting. A door in the back of the house slammed shut.

I turned and looked at Mrs. Peterson. Only then did I notice the purplish welts inside her legs.

"I'm sorry for intruding," I said calmly.

"Don't you people have any decency?" He said to me, then turned on his wife. "And you, Cat. You let him in. How could you? He's representing the *boy* who murdered our Amanda. He's trying to set him *free*."

"But Richard—"

"Shut the fuck up, Cat. You." He turned to me. "Get the fuck out or I'll call the police."

I looked at Cat and she nodded to me. That's when I saw a picture of another girl on the mantle above the fireplace. This one older. She had her arm around her mother and was wearing a blue and white UCI sweatshirt. A third daughter.

I left the way I had come, and he slammed the door shut behind me. I paused a few minutes on the porch but could hear nothing. I had the feeling he was standing behind me, waiting for me to leave.

There was nothing to do but leave.

So I did.

21.

"We should probably call the police," said Cindy, after I told her about my encounter with Richard Peterson. Whom I now referred to as Dick.

"A few bruises and a terrified child does not a case make," I said. "Someone would need to come forward."

She sighed. "And most victims of domestic violence are hesitant to report the abuse, for fear of repercussions."

It was just past 10 p.m. Cindy's evening

class had just ended. We were sitting at a small cafe in the UCI student union. I was eating a chocolate *chocolate* muffin—yes, chocolate chips in a chocolate muffin—the way it should be eaten: big bites that encompassed the stump *and* the top. Cindy was sipping hot cider. The cafe was surrounded by a lot of glass and metal. Couches and chairs lined the walls and filled the many adjoining rooms, filled with students studying and working and *not* making out or sleeping, as I would have done in my day.

"We are surrounded by over-achievers," I said.

"UCI is a tough school to get into," she said. "Same with UCLA. Were you not once an over-achiever?"

"On the football field, yes. In the classroom, my mind wandered."

"Where did it wander?"

"To the next game. The next girl. I was a big man on campus."

She looked at me over her cider. "You still are," she said.

"Are you flirting with me?" I asked.

"If there wasn't a chocolate chip on your chin, the answer would be yes."

She reached over and scooped it off and ate it.

"Does that count against your diet?" I asked.

"I'll jog an extra lap tomorrow morning."

She sat her cider down carefully in front of her. She adjusted the mug so that the handle was facing at a forty-five degree angle. Precision and exactness was her life. And I loved her for it.

I reached over and moved the handle a little to the left.

"Hey," she said, slapping my hand. She adjusted it back. "So what are you going to do about the brute?"

"About Dick? First, I need to speak with the eldest daughter, and confirm my suspicions."

"Your suspicions are generally pretty accurate."

"In this case, I want confirmation. I need to speak to the eldest daughter."

"What's her name?"

"I don't know. I didn't have a chance to ask."

"And how am I supposed to find her here at UCI if you don't know her name?"

"I know her last name is Peterson. Or at least I assume it to be. The other two daughters' names both started with an *A*. So I would begin there. Perhaps an Alicia Peterson, or an Antoinette Peterson."

"You realize this isn't part of your job description, at least not on this case, resolving domestic violence."

"I know."

"And what if she confirms your suspicions of abuse?"

"Then Dick Peterson and I are going to have a talk."

22.

"So why is God dressed like a bum?" I asked. "Isn't that a little cliché?"

"I invented cliché," said Jack.

I rolled my eyes. He continued.

"But to answer your question: This is how you perceive me."

"As a bum?"

"Not exactly. You figure that if God came to earth, he would do so in a nondescript way."

"So as not to attract attention."

"Perhaps."

"So you appeared in just such a way."

"Yes."

"Or maybe you are just a bum, after all."

"Maybe. Either way, you are getting something out of this, am I right?"

I looked at the man. We were sitting opposite each other at the back of the restaurant. At the moment, we were the only two people in McDonald's.

"Yeah, I'm getting something out of it, although I'm not sure what, and I still don't know why you've come into my life."

"You asked me into your life."

"When?"

"The day I first arrived."

I was shaking my head, but then I remembered that day: The twentieth anniversary of my mother's murder. I had spent a good deal of that day cursing God.

"You asked me to come down and face you," said Jack. "I believe you wanted to fight me."

"Yes," I said. "I was very angry."

"And so I came down not to fight you, but to love you, Jim Knighthorse."

"You do this for everybody?"

"Not so dramatically, but often, yes."

"Why me?" I asked.

"Why not?"

I was drinking a Coke. Big, bubbly Coke that was the perfect combination of carbonation, ice and cola. Damn. I love Coke.

"I miss my mother," I said.

"I know, but she has been with you every day of your life."

I suspected that, but didn't say anything about it now.

"You know who killed her?" I asked.

The man in front of me—the *bum* in front of me—nodded once.

"Her case is unsolved," I said.

He watched me carefully.

"And I'm going to solve it," I said. "Some-day."

"Yes," he said, "you will."

"And when I do, I'm going to kill whoever killed her."

Jack said nothing, although he did look away.

23.

I was sitting with my hands behind my head and feet up on one corner of my desk. This is a classic detective pose, and I struck it as often as I could. Mostly because it was a good way to take a nap without appearing to do so. I did my best to keep my shoes off the desktop's gold tooled leather.

There was a knock on my office door. Thanks to Fuck Nut, I kept the door locked these days. I took out my Browning, held it at my hip and opened the door.

The man I found standing before me was perhaps the last person I expected to see. Hell, I hadn't seen or spoken to him in two years. It was my father. His name was Cooper Knighthorse.

***

He studied me for a few seconds, then looked coolly at the gun in my hand. "You could scare off clients with that thing."

"Yeah, well, you're not a client, and someone's sicced a hitman on my ass."

He stood easily six inches shorter than me, which put him around five ten. His shoulders were wider than mine, and he had freakishly large hands, hands which had pummeled my backside more than once. But it was his eyes that drew one's attention. Ice cold and blue. Calculating and fearless. Devoid of anything living. Eyes of a corpse.

He smiled slowly, the lips curling up languidly. When most people smile their eyes crinkle, giving them crow's feet over time. My father would never have to worry about crow's feet. His eyes didn't crinkle. Hell, they didn't know how to crinkle. When he smiled, as he did now, it was only with the corners of his mouth. Needless to say, the smile radiated little warmth.

"Well," he said. "Are you going to invite me in?"

I stepped aside and he moved past me smoothly, carrying himself easily and lightly. He stepped into my four hundred square foot office which paled in comparison to the monster he oversaw in L.A. He stood in the middle of the room, surveying it slowly, taking in the pint-sized refrigerator on one wall, the well-stocked trophy case adjacent to it, my sofa, the sink, and finally the desk.

His assessment was over embarrassingly quick. He turned to face me with no emotion on his face. Did he approve of the place? Or not? Was he proud of his only son, or disappointed? Impossible to tell. Did I need his approval? Impossible to tell. But probably, and it galled me to admit it.

He was wearing a western-style denim shirt and khaki carpenter pants with a hammer loop. There was no hammer in the loop. His evenly-distributed silver hair was perfectly parted to one side. He was the picture of fitness and vitality, health and ruggedness. Just don't look at the eyes.

"So," he said, "who wants you dead?"

I stepped around him, slipped into my lea-ther seat and motioned toward the Mr. Coffee.

He shook his head and eased himself down carefully into one of the three client chairs. The chair, which usually creaked, didn't creak this time.

"Someone wants me to back off a case."

"Any idea who that someone is?"

"Not yet."

"Would be good to know that. Better for your health. Who's the hitman?"

"Older guy, wears a hoop earring. Hell of a shooter. Eyes like a shark." I neglected to say: *eyes like yours*.

My father leaned back a little and allowed his cold eyes to spill across my face. They settled on my damaged ear. "He do your ear?"

"Yes."

"He's one sick motherfucker."

"You know him?"

"Runs a kiddie porn magazine. Would be good for society if he disappeared." He paused. "I can take care of him."

"No."

He studied me for a moment. I refused to turn away from his gaze. "Is he a better shooter than you?" he asked.

"We'll find out."

"Or you can just drop the case," said my father. "And he'll leave you alone."

"Or not."

He smiled. "Or not."

We sat together in silence. Muted street sounds came through the closed window. My refrigerator kicked on and hummed away. My father lifted his gaze without moving his head and scanned the wall behind me. He was looking at the pictures, the articles, the bullet holes in the wall. I could kiss my security deposit goodbye.

"I watched every game," he said.

This was news to me, but I remained silent.

"I was there for every game. At least every home game. I always sat in the back rows. How did you get so goddamn good?"

"Must have been all those special moments we spent playing catch in the park on Sunday afternoons."

"There are some things I regret in this life," he said. "Not being a father to you is one of them." He reached inside his pocket and removed a pouch of photographs. "These were taken on the last day your mother was alive."

Something froze within me, as if my stomach had suddenly been dropped into a bucket of ice. My father, the great Cooper Knighthorse, detective extraordinaire, set the packet on the table.

"I loved her the best way I could, Jim."

"Why are you giving me these pictures?" I

asked.

"Because I want you to see her happy. I want you to see us happy. We were trying, Jim. I was trying."

"You were trying to fuck anything you could get your hands on."

If I shook him, he didn't show it, although the corners of his lips quivered slightly. His pale eyes stared at me.

"We've all made mistakes, Jim. There's something else in the pictures."

"What?"

But he didn't answer me. Didn't even acknowledge my simple question. He simply looked at me a moment longer, stood, then walked out of my office. He shut the door carefully behind him.

I stared at the closed door for a long, long time.

24.

I didn't worry about locking the office door after my father left. I could give a shit about the hitman. I had my Browning on the desk in front of me. Woe to anyone who walked unannounced into my office at that moment.

The packet of photographs was yellowing, the flap torn. On it was a little boy blowing soap bubbles with the word KODAK inside a particularly large bubble. The packet wasn't very thick, containing perhaps twenty-four pictures in all. I had never seen these pictures, and, in fact, did not know of their existence.

I poured myself a cup of coffee with extra cream and sugar.

Heat seeped through the porcelain cup and scalded my palms, but I kept them there, feeling the heat, ignoring the heat, unaware of the heat.

Lifting both hands, I took a sip. Tasted the coffee, but didn't really taste it. Same fucking routine.

I was ten years old when I found her dead. She had bled to death all over her new bedroom set. My father and I had gone to pick up a pizza and rent a movie. I was the first through the front door, carrying the pizza box, excited because my father was in a particularly good mood.

Once inside I called her name, told her the pizza was here and to get it while it was hot. The light was on in her bedroom, but there was no movement, no sound. I set the pizza box down on our dining room table, was about to open it when my father told me to get my mother first.

I headed down the hallway separating the dining room from the master bedroom, calling her name. There was no response. I slowed my pace when I saw her hand lying on the floor. Her hand was completely covered in something red. At first I thought it was a red glove. A wet, gleaming glove, although it wasn't entirely wet. Only parts of it were. It was blood, and it was drying rapidly, congealing over her hand.

I stepped through the doorway and into a nightmare. Blood was everywhere, sprayed across the entire room. It reached everything, touched everything, infused everything. She was lying on the wooden floor in a great puddle of it. Her pink nightgown was soaked. Face-down, her head turned away, looking beneath the bed. The last thing she had seen in the world was a box of my childhood clothing. She kept the box because she always wanted another baby. The box read: Jimmy's Stuff.

There was a bloodied hand print on the box where she had reached for it.

25.

I opened the packet and removed the small pile of pictures. A quick count gave me twenty-two in all.

On the last day of my mother's life, I had been at Pop Warner football practice, and then later at a friend's house for a pool party. I know now my parents had used the opportunity to renew their marriage and spend some quality time together. My mother wanted us to be a happy family. She wanted my father to take an interest in me, rather than viewing me as an obligation. She had gotten pregnant at a young age, and they had married in their late teens. They were not in love.

Early in the marriage, my father joined the military and spent much of that time fighting in secret wars. I would learn later that he was an expert sniper. Expert and deadly. Apparently, my own marksman skills with a gun had been inherited from him. When he came home from his various assignments, flush from his recent kills, he was never really home. He was restless and horny as hell. I had caught him in various parts of town with different women, once in the backseat of our car parked around the corner of our house. I had thrown a brick through the window and scared the hell out of them. I stood there defiantly as he looked up at me through the window. He never said a word about it, never apologized, and had the window replaced the next day.

At first glance, you would never believe that the smiling couple in the picture were unhappy, or that the man with the pale blue eyes was a trained killer or that the woman would only have hours more to live. They were both happy and carefree, hugging and waving. They could have been on a honeymoon.

The majority of the pictures were at the Huntington Beach pier, just a hop skip and jump from my condo. In one picture my mother was sticking her slender backside out seductively toward the camera. My father zoomed in on it tightly. I found myself smiling. They were flirting with each other, and it was nice to see. It was perhaps the most fun I had ever seen them have with each other. For that alone, I was thankful my father had given me the pictures.

He was wearing jeans, carpenter's boots and a yellow T-shirt that said JEEP across it. My mother had on a red blouse, jean shorts and leather sandals. Her legs were slender and naturally tan. Her hair was dark brown and cut short. Her features were slender and sharp. Full red lips and deep brown eyes. She looked like Audrey Hepburn, only prettier.

There were pictures of them along the pier, next to a statue I didn't recognize, standing next to two young men, one of whom was holding a freshly caught sand shark. In that picture, my mother secretly giving my father rabbit ears behind his back.

I went through all of the pictures, my heart heavy and sad. I never recovered from her loss. Mother's Day is hell on me, and I often go into seclusion. How does one replace a mother's love? I lived briefly with an aunt and uncle and they did their best to give me love and attention, but it wasn't the same.

So what else was in the pictures?

What was I missing? What had my father seen that I was missing? Of course, the fact that he had seen it with no prompting was an irritating thought at best.

I went through the pictures again and again, almost setting them aside. Then I found it, and my mouth went immediately dry.

I carefully removed the three photographs and placed them in chronological order on the desktop before me. I noticed my hands were shaking. I linked my fingers together to stop the shaking. I'm not sure it worked.

The first in the series of three pictures was of my parents and the two young men with the sand shark. In the second, my mother was alone and waving to the camera, all smiles, enjoying my father's company for the first time in a long time. Beyond her and up the pier a ways, the two young men with the sand shark were walking away. The brunette dangled the shark over one shoulder, while the bleached blond was looking back toward my mother. The third picture had been near the bottom of the stack, thus near the end of the roll of film, and thus near the end of their day. In that one, my parents were in a souvenir shop in Huntington Beach. The shop was still here to this day. My father had on a goofy baseball cap with a big piece of dog crap on the bill—the hat said *Shit Happens*—while my mother was wearing a colorful straw hat. They were holding each other tight. Behind them was a young man with bleached blond hair. He was watching them, alone this time, about three rows back. He was not smiling, and he did not look too happy.

If I had to guess, I would say he was stalking them.

26.

The sun had set and the ocean was black and eternal.

We were running along the hard-packed sand, passing cuddling lovers who really ought to have gotten a room. There was a dog loose on the beach and I called it over. It followed us briefly, then veered off to chase a hot dog wrapper skimming over the sand. It was humbling to know that we were less interesting than trash.

"So how are you holding up?" Cindy asked.

Her breathing was easy and smooth. She kept pace with me stride for stride.

"My leg?" I asked.

"That and the news about your mother."

"Well, running on sand is a good thing, easy on the leg. As far as my mother," I paused, shrugging. Because I was wearing a nylon coach's jacket, I doubted Cindy could see me shrug, especially in the dark. "I don't know. All I have are a series of pictures featuring a young man who seemed to have taken an inordinate amount of interest in my parents."

"On the day she was murdered."

"Yes."

We were running along an empty stretch of sand now, no lovers or wandering dogs. We were alone with the crashing waves and the black sky. The moon was nowhere to be found; then again, I wasn't looking very hard for it.

"Why did your father give you the pictures now?"

"I don't know."

"Was he keeping them from you for any reason?"

"I don't know."

I was favoring my bad leg, but that was nothing new. Based on the angle and depth of my shoeprints in the sand, a good detective could probably deduce that I had once broken my right leg.

"So what are you going to?"

"There's only one thing to do."

"You're going to look into your mother's murder."

I nodded. "It's something I have always known I would do."

"But you weren't ready yet."

"No."

"Are you ready now?"

"I don't know."

"Has your father looked into her murder?"

"I don't know," I said. "We have never discussed it."

"I think, maybe, it's time that you do."

J.R. RAIN

27.

I was alone in my car overlooking the ocean. I was in a turn-off above the Pacific Coast Highway. Below me was a straight drop of about five hundred feet. My engine was running.

With no leads, my mother's case had been closed. It seemed like another random killing. There had been no sign of sexual trauma, and there were no fingerprints, or blood, other than my mother's. My mother had no known enemies. The only person on the face of the earth that even remotely resented her was my own father. The source of his resentment was me, of course, but we had been together at the time of her murder.

My mother had no family. No brothers or sisters, and both parents were dead. She had only a handful of acquaintances in our neighborhood. In all reality, I was her only family, her only friend, her one true love.

She used to call me her little angel.

I gripped the steering wheel. The leather groaned in my hands. I could hear the blood pounding in my skull. I fought to control my breathing.

After her funeral, she had been all but forgotten. By the police, by her friends, the media, and even her own lackluster husband. She had been forgotten by everyone except me.

I care that you were killed. I care that someone stole your life and cut your throat and hurt you so very badly. I care that you were taken from this earth before your time. I care that you felt the fear of death, the pain of the knife, the hot breath of your killer on your neck. You have not been forgotten, and your little angel is not so little any more.

This was going to take time, I knew. The case was cold. I would investigate it on the side, around my paying work. There was no reason to rush. It's been twenty years, and no one was going anywhere.

J.R. RAIN

28.

The next morning, Sanchez and I were at Cal State Fullerton's defunct football field. The school had spent millions on a fashionable new stadium, hoping to lure big name schools to compete against their smaller program, and then mysteriously decided to pull the plug on football altogether a year later. I sensed a conspiracy.

Still, the bleachers were massive and made for an invigorating stadium workout. It was also hell on my leg. The pain was relentless and disheartening. I was accustomed to my body working through kinks of pain. But this was no kink. This was a pain that encompassed the entire leg. It was a pain that registered in my brain as something *very* wrong, and that perhaps I should stop doing stadiums.

I didn't stop.

I was determined.

Football is all about learning how to live and deal with the pain. Football was in my blood. My father played in college, but he was too small for the pros. I am not too small. I am just right.

Sanchez followed me as we wended our way up and down the narrow concrete stairways between the bleachers. We had been doing this steadily now for thirty-two minutes. I was soaked to the bone. Sanchez had a minor sweat ring around his shirt collar.

The man was a camel.

At thirty-five minutes, my target time, I stopped at the top of the bleachers, gasping for air. Sanchez pulled up next to me, gasping, I was pleased to hear, even louder.

"You need a respirator?" I asked.

"You need a towel?"

We both had our hands on our hips, both wheezing. I had done perhaps ten minutes more than my leg could handle. It was throbbing alarmingly. I tried to ignore it.

We had a great view of Cal State Fullerton's sports complex. I could see the baseball field, built by Kevin Costner, an alumnus of Cal State Fullerton and a hell of a fan and athlete in his own right. Baseball was this little-known university's pride and joy, having won three national championships.

Baseball wasn't a bad sport.

It just wasn't football.

I told Sanchez about Dick Peterson and his daughters. For now, I left news about my mother to myself.

"So you want me to bust this guy?" asked Sanchez when he finally found his wind. "Dick who's-this."

"That would make it worse," I said. "He'll just come back more angry than ever."

"You think he could have killed his own daughter?"

I shrugged. "Anyone who terrifies the youngest one to the point she loses control of her bladder might be capable of doing anything. But he didn't kill her. He was with his wife; they were eating dinner together at the time of the murder."

"So what are you going to do?"

"Talk with the older daughter. Confirm my suspicions."

"And then what?"

The pain in my leg did not subside. It was a constant force. A reminder of what I had lost. But I decided to view it as my one and only obstacle to achieving my goal. It was the only thing standing in my way to becoming what I most wanted. At least, I thought it was what I most wanted. Sometimes the pain made me waver. I hated wavering.

"I will convince him to stop his nefarious ways," I said.

"*Nefarious*," said Sanchez. "Shit. You've been reading too much."

We walked down the bleachers. I could have used a handrail, to be honest.

Sanchez said, "You sure this is all worth it?"

"Yes."

"You're in pain."

"I thought I could hide the pain."

"No one's that good of an actor."

We reached the clay track that surrounded the football field. We were completely alone this morning.

"Why is all this shit you're putting yourself through worth it?"

The morning was still and cool. Steam rose from our bodies. In the distance, on another field, I could see the university's soccer team stretching together.

"It's something left unfinished," I said.

"Maybe some things are meant to be left unfinished."

I thought about that, and had no answer.

29.

After the stadiums I headed straight to 24 Hour Fitness and soaked in their Jacuzzi for half an hour. Now, I was in my office and the pain in my leg was down to a dull throb. I could almost ignore the pain. Almost.

Although my office is in Huntington Beach, it's inland and in a tough area. I fit in nicely here. I grew up in Inglewood, the only white kid in an all black neighborhood, as was my story through elementary school and junior high. It wasn't until I was in high school that I was no longer the only white student. There were five white students at East Inglewood High.

Anyway, I'm at home in tough neighborhoods. Plus the rent's cheaper here.

I sat down in my leather chair and opened a bag of donuts. An NFL fullback weighed anywhere from two-twenty-five to two-fifty. Just to hit the minimum weight I still had to gain another ten pounds. Ideally the weight is added on as muscle and not fat. Well, I had plenty of muscle. I never stopped lifting weights, even for a single day. Except when I was sick, which is different. Your body deserves to rest when sick.

There were five donuts in the bag. I just couldn't bring myself to eat a half dozen. I started on them with a half gallon of whole milk in hand to wash them down. By the third chocolate long john I was beginning to notice a rank smell from within my office. By the time I finished the donuts, the stench was getting worse and I was sure something had died in my office.

I opened a window.

The last thing I wanted to do was disgorge all the precious fat calories I had just consumed. I inhaled some fresh air. My office was on the third floor of a professional building filled with accountants and insurance agents and even a used bookstore that I often perused.

When I was sure I would not launch my donuts into the parking lot below, I turned back into my office, determined to find the source of the stink.

Maybe a possum had died between the walls. Christ, that was going to be a bitch if that were so.

I sniffed away until I found myself back at my desk. Perhaps under? I looked under. Nothing.

I opened my top drawer—and stepped back.

It was there in my drawer. A cat. It had not died of natural causes. No, it had been cut neatly in half, just under the rib cage. A black cat with a cute little blue bell around its neck. Paws were thrown up over its head, like a referee giving the touchdown signal. Its eyes were wide, and it appeared devoid of blood. Just skin, fur and bones.

Tinker Bell.

A piece of greasy paper, stained with ichor and other bodily fluids, was neatly folded and shoved into its chest cavity. I extracted it carefully, and unfolded it. There were just three words on the note:

Last warning,
Meow.

And that's when my fax machine turned on,

startling me. Shaken, I got up, leaving the severed cat where it lay in my drawer. The fax was from Cindy. It was a short list of three names, all of them *A. Petersons* from UCI. Their class schedules were included. The last faxed page was a photocopy of Cindy's small palm pressed down against the glass of the copy machine. Written below her palm were the words: *I like your touch.*

I needed that.

30.

I went to Huntington High in search for clues. That is, after all, what detective do. In particular I went searching for someone, *anyone*, who might be able to corroborate Derrick's story.

It was almost 7:00 p.m., about the time Amanda had been murdered. I wanted to see what kind of staff was on hand at the witching hour.

I cruised through the faculty parking lot, which ran along the west side of the school. It was nearly empty, just six vehicles in total. The student parking lot was fuller, but that could be the result of the outdoor basketball courts and tennis courts that were nearby. The days were longer now than when Amanda was murdered two months ago, so I expected to see more activity in and around the school.

At the moment, the sun was just setting, and much of the school was in shadow. Outdoor lights, many of them flickering chaotically, were perched along the upper corners of the many buildings. A security truck was parked in the visitor's parking lot near the main entrance. There was someone inside, a large black man, talking on a cell phone. Huntington High was one of the few schools in the area that did not lock down their campus at night, trusting instead to a few tough-looking security guards.

I parked three spaces from the truck, and so that I was official, I clipped my visitor badge to the pocket of my T-shirt. As I stepped out of my car, I had the full attention of the security guard by now. He leaned out the driver's side window and beckoned me toward him. I showed him the visitor's badge by sticking out my considerable chest. Perhaps too impressed for words by the size of my chest, he simply nodded once and leaned back in his front seat.

I headed up to the school along a wide

concrete path. The main hall was deserted. My sneakers echoed dully off the many lockers. Further along I heard whistling from some-where. Had I been a puppy dog, my ears would have shot forward, twitching nervously. Unfortunately I wasn't a puppy dog, though certainly as cute, and did my human best to zero in on the sound.

I turned a corner and came to a bathroom. A girl's bathroom.

A janitor's cart was parked out front, filled with cleaners and rags and brooms. Draped over a broom handle was a sweat-stained Anaheim Angel's baseball cap. The whistler was whistl-ing something I did not recognize, although it sounded sort of mournful. Something you might hear on death row, perhaps.

White light issued from that most hallowed of places: the girl's bathroom, where periods were discovered, cigarettes smoked and boys gossiped about. At least hallowed to the minds and considerable imaginations of high school boys.

I rapped loudly on the open door.

The whistling stopped. A man's head jerked around the corner of one of the stalls, eyes wide with alarm, as if he had been caught doing something. Whatever it was he was doing, I didn't want to know. He was Hispanic, dark complexion, wide brown eyes. Perhaps forty-five. His forehead glistened with sweat.

"Hi," I said, ever the friendly stranger.

He said nothing. His sewn-on name badge said Mario.

"Do you speak English, Mario?"

He nodded. I held up my badge proclaiming me as an official visitor. He relaxed a little. I stepped into the bathroom and he flinched. I handed him one of my cards, holding it before him, until he finally tore his gaze off me and took the card. He looked at it carefully.

"Nice picture, huh?" I said. I turned my head to the right and gave him the same smile that was on the card.

"You...you a private detective?" he said in strangled English.

"The very best this side of the Mississippi. Just don't tell my pop that. He hates competition."

He looked at me expressionlessly.

"Never mind," I said. "Can I ask you a few questions?"

He shrugged, which was the correct response if my question was taken literally. I dunno, his shrug seemed to say, *can* you ask me a question?

"Much work to do," he said.

"I bet."

I reached inside my pocket and gave him a hundred dollar bill. He took it without realizing what he was reaching for. Then he shook his head vigorously and tried to give it back.

"Keep it," I said.

"No, *señor*."

He thrust it back into my pocket. Sometimes money talks, sometimes it doesn't. I asked, "Were you here on the night Amanda Peterson was murdered?"

He blinked up at me. Whether or not he understood I didn't know.

I forged bravely ahead. "On the night Amanda Peterson was murdered, could you verify whether or not Derrick Booker was in the school's weight room?"

He said nothing. Sweat had broken out on his brow. He was looking increasingly troubled. "Please, *señor*. I know nothing." His voice was pleading, filled with panic.

I studied him, watching his agitated body movements, and on a hunch I asked, "Has someone else been here to speak with you?" I asked. "An older man, perhaps? Gray hair, an earring." I gestured to my ear. "A golden hoop?"

He was gasping for breath. "Please, *señor*. He scare my family."

Bingo. I walked over to him and took my

card from his trembling hands and placed it carefully in his overall's pocket at his chest.

"I'm going to take care of him, Mario. I promise."

He said nothing. We stared at each other. His eyes were wide and white.

The hitman had come to see him. Warned him to shut up. Threatened his family. No wonder Mario was terrified.

"It's going to be alright, Mario. No one's going to hurt you or your family."

He said nothing more.

I left the way I had come.

31.

The day was bright and there was a chill to the air, but that did not stop eighty-three percent of the female college students at UCI from wearing tiny shorts and cut-off T-shirts that revealed many pierced belly buttons.

I had already tried one of the classrooms, using the schedule Cindy had faxed me, but I did not see a single young lady who looked like the framed picture on the Peterson's mantle.

Now I was standing outside a classroom in the Humanities building. I was on the seventh floor and had a great shot of what the students here called Middle Earth, a beautiful central park located within the campus.

One of the problems I was running into were that many of the girls *could* have been *A. Peterson*. Hell, most of them were cute with dark hair.

"Excuse me," said a voice behind me.

I turned away from the window. I saw that the class across the hall had just let out, and I had already missed a few faces. Damn. But standing in front of me was clearly A. Peterson. Cute face, cute button nose. But the cuteness ended there. Everything else about the girl was anything but cute.

"Miss Peterson?"

She nodded, frowning. "Are you the private investigator that came to see my mom?"

She looked haunted. No. She *was* haunted. Her pale eyes were empty, troubled and suspicious. A heavy backpack weighed her down, and she was hunched forward to support some of the weight. Her arms were crossed in front of her, her hands holding her bony shoulders. Her hair was dyed pitch black, skin pale and milky. She had a nose, tongue and brow ring. Had she decided to wear make-up, she would have been able to cover the dark rings around her eyes.

"How did you know me?" I asked.

"My mom described you. She called me last night. Said a tall muscular man with a full head of blond hair and a tattoo of a black horse on his forearm had come to see her about Amanda." Her voice was soft and wispy. I strained to listen to her.

"And I fit the description?"

She looked at my crossed arms. The black horse, shooting steam from its nostrils, was clear on my left forearm.

"Plus," she said, "You're packing heat."

She pointed to the bulge under my left armpit. I was leaning against the wall in such a way that the bulge was evident to those who knew where to look.

"You would make a hell of an investigator," I said.

"Investigative journalism is my major."

"I couldn't think of a more fitting job," I said. "What's your name?"

"Annette," she said.

"Ah," I said.

"And you found my classroom, so you're not so bad yourself." She might have grinned, but she had probably forgotten how.

"Glad I have your vote of confidence."

"I assume you're here to talk with me about my sister?"

"Yes," I said. "That and more. Is there somewhere we can have privacy?"

32.

We were in Middle Earth, surrounded by oaks and pines and a lot of rolling green hills. Students with laptops were banging away under trees nearby. Other students were soaking in the sun, and too few were making out. There was one couple, however, going at it like minks. Good for them. College at its best.

We were sitting on the grass. My back was up against the trunk of a gnarled ash tree, and Annette was leaning against her massive backpack which was filled to overflowing.

"Are you a senior?" I asked.

"Yes."

"Do you live at home?"

She shook her head vehemently. "I needed to get away. Far away. But I couldn't leave mother and my sisters. So I compromised with my mother. I live in a dorm here at UCI, and my sisters and mother can come visit me anytime."

I said, "Your father is abusive." It wasn't a question.

"Do you know where my mom called me from last night?"

I had a sinking feeling. "The hospital."

She nodded. "You are good. Two broken ribs and a broken nose. Said she fell down the stairs. We don't have fucking stairs."

"Shit."

"Shit is right. The man is a goddamn animal and I have hated him my entire life."

"He abuse you?"

"Often."

"Sexually?"

"No. Not me. I wouldn't let him. I fought him. So he settled on beating the shit out of me. Broke my arm twice. In the same fucking place. Loves to grab it and shake until something snaps."

"Were your sisters sexually abused?"

"I think so, and I'm pretty sure little Alyssa

is getting the worst of it now, especially now that she's alone with him."

"Has your mother ever tried to leave?"

"No. He tells her he will kill her and her daughters. Classic shit. She's terrified of him."

"Has anyone ever gone to the police? Have any teachers ever noticed the bruises, questioned your broken arms?"

"The answer is no. Father is an assemblyman for the county. He can have anyone's job. He knows it and they know it. Our plight has been ignored."

"Plight," I said, grinning at her. "You must be a writer."

"Someday soon I hope to even make money at it."

"Would you like your father to stop the abuse?"

"Of course. Stupid fucking question." She leaned forward, hands flat in the grass. Not surprisingly, her nails were unpainted. "Are you going to stop him?"

I shrugged. "I could give a shit if he's an assemblyman. I work for myself. I could make most men on this earth bend to my will."

She actually laughed and clapped, and that pretty much made my day. She said, "That's such a funny way to describe that you are going to royally kick his ass."

"Royally."

"He's a big guy," she said. "But you're bigger."

"I'm bigger than most. And if I happen to break his arm in the process?"

Her gaze hardened. "Tell him it was from me."

A Frisbee landed next to us. I flicked it back to an embarrassed young lady. She caught it neatly with one hand and dashed off.

"One more thing," I said. "Do you know why Amanda quit her school band?"

"Because the band director was a creep."

"How do you know?"

"He made a pass at her," she said.

"What did she do about it?"

"Told him to leave her alone."

"I assume he didn't."

"No."

"And then she quit?" I asked.

"Yes."

"Did she often confide in you?" I asked.

She looked away. "Yeah, we were close."

"I'm sorry," I said.

"So am I."

I gave her one of my cards, and she looked at it.

"Nice picture, Mr. Knighthorse," she said.

"I know."

33.

It was early morning and the crowd in McDonald's consisted mostly of old men in tan shorts, white tee shirts and running shoes. Most didn't look like they did much running.

I was eating a Big Breakfast with Jack at the back of the restaurant. He was sipping his lukewarm black coffee and looking very ungod-like in his bum outfit. Then again, according to him, this is how I expected him to look.

"So who's running the universe if you're down here with me?"

"I can be in many places."

"Convenient," I said. "Must make waiting in line for Zeppelin tickets a breeze."

"And makes doing chores a snap."

"Was that a joke?" I asked.

"Yes."

"God jokes?"

"Who do you think invented humor?"

"The devil?" I asked.

"There is no devil, you know that."

"I know that because you told me there's no devil. I'm still not convinced."

The man in front of me shrugged and sipped his coffee. I've noticed that Jack often didn't care if I believed him or not. I found that interesting and a little disconcerting.

"Prove to me you're God."

"Prove I'm not."

"Touché," I said. "What's the square root of one million?"

"Do you know?"

"No," I said. "But I will later."

"Then ask me later."

"Fine," I said. "Perform a miracle. A real miracle."

"Like turning coffee into wine?"

"Yes. That. Or beer. Turn it into ice cold beer and let me drink it."

"You sound like an alcoholic, Jim."

"You would know."

"Drinking is not good for your body. In fact, it's very hard on your body."

"Let's not go down that road."

"Okay," he said. "What road would you like to go down?"

"I want a miracle. I want proof that I'm talking to God."

"One man's miracle is another man's reality."

"Oh, screw that," I said. "Turn something into something else, and quit giving me shit."

"And if I performed a miracle for you, that would finally satisfy your curiosity?"

"Yes."

"No it wouldn't. You would ask for another miracle, and then another. Always doubting."

"You're not going to perform a miracle, are you?"

"No. That is, not in the way that you mean."

"But you perform other miracles?"

"Every day. Every second."

"But if you performed a miracle for me now, then I would no longer have to believe, or have to have faith."

"This is true."

"I think faith is overrated. Turn something into something else and I will be your biggest follower, I promise."

"I don't want a follower. I just want you to listen, to think for yourself and to lead the best life you can. Ultimately, to define who you are and to live by those convictions."

"And if you performed a miracle for me..."

"Then you will no longer make your own choices."

"I would blindly do whatever you say," I said.

"Yes. Exactly."

"But you are here now, claiming to be God."

"Like I said, one man's miracle—"

"Is another man's reality," I finished.

We were silent some more. I looked in his half-empty cup. It was still coffee.

Jack closed his eyes, seemed to have fallen asleep, but he did this often, going to wherever God goes.

"Everything okay?" I asked.

"Very."

"I'm going to hurt a man," I said.

"Do what you must."

"Really?"

"I do not define for you what is right or wrong."

"Au contraire," I said. "There's a whole book out there that defines exactly what we sho-uld do."

"Was that French?" he asked.

"Oh shut up," I said. "Wait, did I just tell God to shut up?"

"Yes. Would you like for me to shut up?"

"No."

"Remember, I will not tell you how to lead your life, nor will I tell you what decisions to make, or who or what defines you. These are your choices. Your gifts. The book or books of which you refer, were often inspired by me, but only the parts about love."

"Love?"

"As in do all things with love."

"All things?"

"Yes," he said. "This concept alone would change much of the structure of your planet."

"There are those who can't love, or choose not to love."

"There are those," said Jack, "who are an unfortunate byproduct of your current state of non-loving."

"You do realize we are in a McDonald's?"

"Yes."

"Am I going crazy?" I asked.

"That is for you to decide."

"So you really do not care if I hurt another human being?"

"Do you derive pleasure from hurting others, Jim?"

"No. I will be hurting another to protect

many more."

"Are you living and acting and behaving within your own moral standards?"

"Yes."

"Is this what defines who you are?"

"Yes."

"And so you are being true to yourself?"

"I guess so, yes."

"I can find no fault in that."

"So you approve?" I asked.

"I approve of defining who you are, Jim. There is a difference. And there are many, many people out there who do not have a strict moral code, such as your own."

"So any moral code would work?"

"Any *true* moral code, Jim," said Jack. "Any true code."

34.

Sanchez and I waited in Sanchez's unmarked police vehicle in a red zone across the street from the offices of Assemblyman Richard Peterson.

"His name has a nice ring to it," said Sanchez.

We were in the city of Brea, in a shopping zone that called itself Downtown Brea. The stores were all new, and there was not one but two movie theaters. The apartments above the stores were advertised as artists' lofts. Once, long ago, I wanted to be an artist, until I realized I wasn't good enough and didn't have enough patience.

"There are two ice cream shops," said Sanchez. "I wonder why."

"They are across the street from each other," I said. "Downtown Brea is all about convenience."

"If you say so."

"There's our man."

It was past 6:30 p.m. and Richard Peterson was just leaving the office. He was leaving with a rather pretty blond in a short red dress. She split one way, walking to a nearby restaurant bar, and blew him a little kiss.

"Maybe she's the secretary," I said.

"Bet she takes great dictation."

Peterson crossed the street purposefully, and headed to the parking structure to our right. We watched him ascend the stairs.

"Takes the stairs. Keeps in shape," said Sanchez. "You think you can handle him?"

"As long as he doesn't take them two at a time."

We waited at the mouth of the structure's exit, and sure enough a black Escalade with Peterson at the helm came tearing through the structure, heedless of babies or speed bumps.

"I could give him a ticket for reckless

driving," said Sanchez.

"For now just follow him."

Sanchez did, pulling in behind him. Peterson drove like a man drunk or on drugs, weaving carelessly in and out of traffic.

"At least he uses his blinker," I said.

"Considerate. Where do you want this to go down?"

We were on a street called Brea Blvd. The street was wide and quiet.

"This is good," I said.

Sanchez, hidden behind his cop glasses, reached under his seat and pulled out a flashing light with a magnetized bottom. He put it on top of his vehicle. I saw Peterson jerk his head up and look in the rearview mirror a couple of times. Finally he yanked the Escalade off to the side of the road. Sanchez pulled in behind him.

I said, "You don't have to do this. He's my problem. You could get into a lot of trouble."

"Justice is justice, Knighthorse. Sometimes street justice can be more effective."

"And less paperwork."

"And less paperwork," said Sanchez. "Wait here."

35.

I watched from the passenger seat. Sanchez spoke with Peterson through the open window. A moment later I heard a lot of shouting, saw a lot of gesticulating, then the Escalade door burst open and Peterson came charging out. He waggled a finger in Sanchez's face. From here, his finger looked like a worm on a hook.

Sanchez said something and Peterson reluctantly turned and put both hands on the SUV's hood.

I watched intently.

Sanchez was an old pro. He kicked Peterson's feet apart and patted him down. Peterson said something over his shoulder and Sanchez pushed him hard against the fender. I heard the thump from here. Peterson's sunglasses fell from his face.

Sanchez removed a pair of handcuffs from his belt, twisted Peterson's arm back, then cuffed the assemblyman's wrist. The whole cuffing process took less than three seconds, faster than Peterson could react. Once he realized what had happened, he swung around violently. Sanchez stepped back, removed his gun and pointed it at Peterson's chest.

Peterson backed off, breathing hard. Sanchez walked him back to the vehicle.

And just like that we kidnapped Mr. Richard Peterson, Orange County Assemblyman, wife beater and child molester.

***

He shoved Peterson in the backseat. I took off my shades and turned around.

"Hi, Dick," I said. "Dick is an acceptable variant of Richard, am I correct?"

Recognition dawned on Peterson's red and sweaty face. His eyes narrowed and his pupils shrank. "It's *you*. The *detective*. What the fuck is going on?"

I turned to Sanchez. "Do you want me to quiet him up for the ride out?"

"Go ahead, I'm tired of hearing him already."

I stepped out of the front seat, opened the back door, and punched Peterson as hard as I could. Even from my awkward angle, the blow was still a good one and caught him sharply across the temple, snapping his head around.

Dazed, he didn't go unconscious, but it sure shut him up.

I turned and headed toward the Escalade.

"Follow me," I said to Sanchez.

***

I followed a street called Carbon Canyon through the city of Brea. Soon the new homes and the massive state park disappeared and we were on a winding road. The Escalade drove like a dream. Shame what was going to happen to it.

I found a dirt turn-off and hung a right. In my rearview mirror, Sanchez followed me closely, although he didn't use his turn blinker. Damn cops. Above the law. First kidnapping, and now this.

We were now following a small creek, and

when we reached a point where the creek dropped off twenty feet below down a dirt embankment, I stopped the Cadillac.

Sanchez pulled up behind me with Peterson in the backseat. I put the Escalade in neutral, and stepped outside. With Sanchez's help, we pushed the Cadillac down the dirt embankment. It ricocheted nicely off two trees, careened off a pile of boulders, and then splashed down in the middle of the creek, hissing and steaming.

The vehicle was totaled.

"Damn shame," said Sanchez.

"Yep."

36.

"Let him go," I said to Sanchez.

Sanchez uncuffed Peterson. The assembly-man was still woozy from the blow to the head. His hair was ruffled and his face was red, and it looked like he might have been missing a button on his shirt. He looked from me to Sanchez, and then at his surroundings. Dawning seemed to come over him as he realized he was not in a good situation. When he spoke, there was real fear in his voice, along with much nastiness.

"Do you have any idea who I am?" he

asked.

"You are Richard Peterson, county assemblyman and respected citizen. You are also a wife beater and a child abuser who rapes his own children. Is there anything I missed?"

He looked at me briefly, then lumbered over to the creek and looked down at his Escalade. "You can't prove any of it," he said, still looking down. He might have considered bolting if he wasn't still dazed.

"I'm not here to prove anything."

"So what's going on? You want money to keep everything quiet?"

Sanchez laughed and leaned a hip against the fender of his vehicle.

"No," I said. "You have been tried and found guilty, Mr. Peterson. Now comes the punishment phase. I will allow you to defend yourself."

"It's two against one, hardly fair."

"My compatriot is here for entertainment purposes only."

"*Compatriot?*" said Sanchez.

"Yeah."

Peterson sized me up, eyes darting quickly. Sweat was on his brow, and spreading quickly under his pits.

"You're bigger than me."

"I'm bigger than most."

"Not me," said Sanchez.

"We're even," I said to Sanchez. "Besides, we've already had this argument before, which is why I said *most*."

I turned back to Peterson. He backed up. If he bolted and was fast enough I could be in trouble with my gimp leg. Sanchez pulled out his gun and pointed it at Peterson again.

"No running," said Sanchez.

"You didn't give your children a chance to run, did you?" I asked. "When you beat them or forced yourself on them."

"What the *fuck* is going on?"

"I am here for two things: first, to convince you of the error of your ways, and second to convince you to, um, give up the error of your ways."

"Poetic," said Sanchez.

"Shut up, I'm making this up as I go."

"I can tell," said Sanchez.

I said to Peterson, "I am going to kick the royal shit out of you. You are going to have a beating unlike anything you've ever had in your life. You will tell the authorities you suffered your injuries in a car accident, resulting from your desire to go sightseeing. You will stick to this story or a letter written by your daughter Annette detailing your sexual tendencies toward your own children will be mailed instantly to all the local papers. Do you understand?"

He stared at me blankly, sweating. He looked like he needed a drink of water.

"And if you ever so much as lay a finger on your wife or children again, your next car accident will be your last. Are we clear?"

"Lesson learned, I swear. I mean, hell, you've scared the shit out of me. I'm practically peeing my pants here."

"*Practically*," I said to Sanchez. "Then I'm not doing my job."

"Losing your touch," said Sanchez.

"Put your gun away," I told Sanchez.

Sanchez did and continued grinning and watching us. A squirrel ran along a tree branch overhead. We were far from Carbon Canyon Road. The air was fresh and scented with moss and soil and pine.

"I will give you a chance to fight back, which is more than you deserve."

"Fuck you, asshole," he said.

"That's the spirit."

He looked from me to Sanchez, and then took his shot, his right hand lashing out. I maneuvered myself in time to take the majority of the blow off my shoulder. I countered with something like a jab, which broke his nose.

"Fuck," he said, holding the bleeding mess.

Next, I did what I do best. I tackled him low.

It was a quick movement that combined my football and wrestling skills. He landed hard on his back, and his air whooshed from his lungs like an escaping devil.

I hauled Peterson up and walked him over to Sanchez's car and placed his left forearm on the fender.

"You broke Annette's arm. Twice."

"Fuck you," he said, holding his nose and gasping. "The bitches deserved everything they got. Fuck you and fuck them."

I broke his arm quickly, bringing my elbow down hard on his wrist. The snap reverberated throughout the woods. Birds erupted from nearby tree branches.

Sanchez looked away.

Peterson cried out, grabbed for his arm.

But I wasn't done with him.

No, not by a long shot.

I went to work on him, and when it was finally over, when Sanchez finally pulled me off him, my knuckles were split and bloodied and I was gasping for breath.

37.

The MGD bottle slipped from my fingers and crashed to my cement balcony. Foam erupted among the broken glass shards.

Shit.

I considered grabbing another beer from the twenty-four pack at my feet, then decided to give it a rest for the night. Instead, I began drunkenly counting the empty glass bottles standing like sentries along the tabletop, lost count, started over, lost count again, then decided that I had drunk a shit-load of beer tonight.

I had murders, child molesters, broken arms, dead cats, suicides and death threats on my mind. And now perhaps new information about my mother. Enough to drive any man to drink. But then again I never needed much reason to drink.

Cindy was with her sister-in-law tonight, Francine. They got together once every other week and gossiped about their men, football and the nature of God in society since Francine was a religious studies instructor at Calabasas Junior College near San Diego.

That left me alone tonight. Just me and my beer.

I automatically reached down for another beer. Stopped halfway. Put my hands in my lap, and laced my fingers together.

Good boy.

The night was cool; a soft breeze swept over my balcony. Traffic was thick on PCH. I could smell exhaust and grilling hamburgers.

On its own accord, my hand reached down for another bottle. I stopped it just as it brushed a cold bottle cap.

The bone had snapped loud enough for birds to erupt in surprise.

My knuckles still ached from the beating I gave Peterson. The assemblyman's solo vehicle accident had made the local papers. Neither I nor Sanchez were mentioned. After the beating, we had dragged Peterson's limp body down the incline and stowed him in the driver's seat. I placed a call via his cell phone to 911, pretending to be Peterson, gasping in pain. Hell of a performance. Sanchez was amused, although I noted he looked a little sick and pale.

A horn honked from below, along Main Street, followed by a short outburst of obscenities.

I would have killed Peterson if Sanchez hadn't pulled me off him.

And, Lord help me, I was enjoying every minute of it.

I reached down and grabbed another beer. This time there was no stopping my hand. I twisted off the cap and drank from it. And it was good, so very, very good.

J.R. RAIN

38.

"How's the case going?" asked Cindy.

She had just sat down in front of me at the Trocadero, a Mexican place across the street from UCI. She was wearing a casual business suit, and her hair was down. She looked three years my junior, rather than the other way around. Her lipstick was bright red, which was good since I was color blind. Seriously. She wore the bright red for me.

"Other than the fact that I have no idea who killed Amanda, just swell."

The waiter took our drink orders. An apple martini for Cindy and Coke for me.

"I called you last night," she said. "Twice."

"I know," I said, "and I called you this morning when I got the messages."

She let her unspoken question hang in the air: *so why didn't you pick up?* I let it hang in the air as well. I still felt like shit from the night before. I had drunk the entire case. A new record for me.

"Are you feeling well?" she asked.

"Just great."

"Bullshit. Your eyes are red and you look pale." She opened her purse and removed the local edition of the Orange County Register. "Amanda Peterson's father was in an accident. A bad accident. A broken arm. Three broken ribs. A broken collar bone. And a broken jaw. Jesus Christ, Jim."

"Like they said, a bad accident."

"It was no accident."

"No," I said, looking at her. "It wasn't; it was a methodical beating that I gave to a son-of-a-bitch to reinforce the idea that he is to never, *ever* touch his family inappropriately again. The way I see it, he got off easy. His wounds will heal. The damage he inflicted may never heal."

"Did your point hit home?" There might

have been sarcasm in her voice.

"So far he's sticking to the accident story. So he's scared. As he should be."

The waiter came around and took our order. Salmon for Cindy and two Super Mex chicken burritos for me, extra guacamole and sour cream.

"You're going to kill yourself before your tryouts," said Cindy. More sarcasm?

"I'm still about seven pounds from my target weight."

"Isn't there a healthier way to gain weight?"

"Is that an oxymoron?"

"I'm serious, Jim. I'm concerned about you. About us."

She wouldn't look me in the eye, and sipped her martini faster than normal. Her free hand played with the napkin, repeatedly wadding it and smoothing it out.

"What's wrong?" I asked.

"I can't keep doing this."

"You mean strangling your napkin?"

"No. I mean us."

I let the air out of my lungs. We had had this conversation before.

"Last time, I convinced you to stay," I said. "Talked until I was blue in the face. Do you remember what I told you I would do if you did this to me again?"

"Yes," she said. "You said you wouldn't try to stop me the next time."

"Yes."

The napkin was wasted, rendered perfectly useless. She pushed it aside and drank deeply from her martini. So deeply, in fact, that she finished it. I said nothing. There was nothing for me to say. I was not going to keep having this conversation with her. I loved Cindy with all of my heart, but I was not going to make her do something she did not want to do.

The waiter saw her empty glass and came over.

"Another?" he asked.

"Yes, please."

She still hadn't looked me in the eye. I studied her closely. She was behaving very un-Cindy like. Small, jerky movements as she tapped on the now empty cardboard coaster. She wiped her mouth with the back of her hand.

I said nothing.

"Jesus Christ, Jim, you beat the unholy shit out of another human being. Your life has been threatened by a hired killer. A dead cat shows up in your office. Cut in fucking *two*. And now you're drinking again. It's not that you're drinking, really. It's that you are getting drunk, and doing it in secret, which makes it dirty and dangerous and all-consuming. And, ultimately, sad. Very, very sad."

I said nothing.

"You didn't answer the phone last night because you were passed out."

Her second apple martini came, followed by a second waiter bearing our food. The food was placed before us; it went ignored.

"And now you're trying out for the Chargers in a few weeks. What if you make the team? I would never see you. I know that's selfish of me, but it's true. You would throw your whole life into it, like you do everything else, and the NFL would own your heart and soul. Would there be any room left for me?"

She drank her martini. Her eyes were wet. Hands shaking. She spilled some of the drink, and used the shredded napkin to clean up. The napkin only managed to smear the liquid.

"Christ, aren't you going to say anything?"

I said nothing.

"And I love you so much, you big sonofabitch. You worked your way deep into my heart like a damn thorn. A thorn that hurts, but has so much love to give."

I didn't like the analogy, but said nothing.

"I worry so much about you. But you can take care of yourself. I've seen it. And you have Sanchez and your father to help you. The three of you are an amazingly formidable force. And you are so brutal and deadly, but moral and just, and so fucking hilarious. Shit."

She stopped talking and picked at her salmon. She even went as far as to bring up a forkful, but then got distracted by her own thoughts, and set it down again.

"You are a wonderful man, but you fuck me up."

She started crying. She brought her hands to her face, and the tears leaked from under her palms. I resisted the strong urge to reach out to her. She needed to make a decision. I was not going to influence her decision in any way. I held on to that thought, no matter how hard it was for me to do so.

"Are you just going to sit there and let me cry?"

I said nothing, and didn't move, although my hand flinched.

"I think I need to leave," she said.

She did, getting up quickly and dashing through the dark restaurant. I watched her go, and when she was gone I set aside my Coke and signaled the waiter.

I was going to need something a little stronger.

39.

It was almost 1:00 a.m. when I came home that night.

With a twelve-pack of MGD in hand, I took the stairs two at a time, climbing my way to the fifth floor, where my apartment and drinking sanctuary awaited. I had made it a point recently to always take the stairs, to augment my training. I figured every little bit helped.

I was regretting that decision now. Especially at this hour, and what had happened over dinner.

Maybe I should have said something to her, I thought.

But I was determined not to sway her decision. She needed to decide for herself whether or not she wanted me in her life. Me prostrating myself, switching into used car salesman mode, and listing my strengths and perks did no one any good. It debased me on one level, and clouded her thinking on another.

Cindy and I had been seeing each other steadily since my senior year in college. At the time, she was in the master's program at UCLA. I had met her through a teammate of mine, her brother Rob. Cindy had come from a football family, and although she made no real effort to understand the sport, she at least understood the men who played it, and we were a good match. She went on to get her doctoral in anthropology, her expertise the anthropology of world religions. Turns out, there's a lot of world religions out there, and so she keeps fairly busy writing papers and what-nots. She's only recently been tenured at UCI, which is great because now she really has to royally screw up to be fired. Luckily, she rarely screws up.

After my injury, she had been so supportive during those years of rehabilitation. She had also been supportive of the idea of me following in the footsteps of my father, although I had sworn long ago to never be a detective. I mean, I was destined for a long and rewarding career in football, right? Say ten years in the NFL, another ten in broadcasting, and finish things up as an NFL coach. That had been the plan.

Things change.

Especially when you're hit by a cheap chop block, and you hear the sound of your bones fracturing in so many places that you still have nightmares over it. It was only later, after my drinking had started, that I found amusement in the fact that the fracturing of my leg had sounded like the popping of popcorn.

I was now on the fifth floor. I was not winded, but there was a healthy burn in my legs. And as I stepped through the stairwell door, I saw a man smoking a cigarette five feet away. He was waiting by the elevator door, and there was a pistol hanging loosely by his side. He did not see me.

It was Fuck Nut.

40.

I eased the stairwell door shut, removed the Browning from my shoulder holster and set down the beer. This wing of the fifth floor is reserved for four apartment suites. The elevator lets you out under a veranda outdoors. From there one can choose four different routes: immediate right or left, or straight ahead and then right or left. My apartment was straight ahead and then right. The whole area is flooded with outdoor lighting.

He had been leaning behind a stucco pillar,

just feet from the elevator, gun hanging idly by his side, blowing smoke from his cigarette straight into the air. I could smell the smoke.

I had the element of surprise, of course, being that he did not expect anyone in their right mind to walk up five flights of stairs, especially someone with a bum leg. And if Fuck Nut was a professional killer, as I assumed him to be, he had done his research on me; he knew about the bum leg. He was confident I would take the elevator. He did not realize I was a hell of an example of human perseverance in the face of tragedy.

In the least he should have positioned himself to see the stairs and elevator.

Expect the unexpected, as my father would say.

I eased open the door and raised the Browning.

But he was no longer standing behind the pillar. No, he was now waiting off to the side of the elevator. His cigarette, tossed aside, was glowing ten feet away, half finished.

Because the elevator door was about to open.

Shit.

He raised his own weapon. In the glow of the outdoor lights I could see he had a silencer on the end of his pistol. A true killer.

The doors slid open.

Yellow light from the elevator washed across the veranda, and out stepped my Indian neighbor from across the way. My neighbor who had told me his name seven or eight times but I could never remember it. Poorjafar? I always felt like crap asking him to pronounce his name again, so we both accepted the fact that he was known as "Hey!" And I was known as "Jeemmy!" Normally, *Jeemmy* is an unacceptable variant of my name, but I let it slide in this case.

The man who might be Poorjafar was a big guy who lifted weights, and he stepped confidently out of the elevator, swirling his key ring on his finger and whistling. I didn't recognize the song, but it had a sort of Bollywood feel to it. And, for effect, Poorjafar stopped, did a little dance, turned around—

And saw the hitman.

"Oh, shit," said Poorjafar, stepping back, startled.

Fuck Nut said nothing.

"Are you waiting for someone?" asked my neighbor.

"You could say that," said the hitman.

I knew something about assassins. They didn't like witnesses. They saw themselves as living outside the real world; in fact it was a fantasy world of their construct, where they were king and God, pronouncing life and death on mere mortals.

The killer had just pronounced death on Poorjafar.

There would be no witnesses tonight, if the killer had his way.

I stepped out of the stairwell, losing my element of surprise, my own gun hidden behind my back. "He's waiting for me," I said.

Poorjafar turned. "Jeemmy! How you doing, man?"

"Hey...*hey*."

Poorjafar pointed at the man in the shadows. "This is a friend of yours?"

The killer didn't move, but his eyes wanted to bug out of his skull. He shifted uneasily, but kept his gun out of sight. I kept my eyes on him.

"He's a recent acquaintance," I said.

"Well, your acquaintance scared the shit out of me."

"Yeah, he likes to do that. Of course, it doesn't help that he's such an ugly bastard." I gave a big, fake hearty laugh. The killer didn't laugh. "Probably scared the shit out of his own mother when he was born."

Poorjafar laughed, and I could smell the alcohol on his breath.

"Shit, Jeemmy. That was a low blow. He's a

friend, man."

"No, I'm not," said the man. "I'm very much not his friend."

And he stepped sideways, keeping his hand behind his back, and stepped into the elevator. He pressed a button; the door closed. He pointed a finger at me and fired a blank bullet. And he was gone. I went back for my beer, and Poorjafar danced and whistled his way into his apartment.

J.R. RAIN

41.

I was at East Inglewood High, my old high school, practicing hitting drills with my even older high school football coach. Twelve years ago I made a name for myself on this field, where I was loved and worshipped. Isn't football just swell?

Coach Samson was a big black man, now in his fifties, and I still feared him on some level. But more than fear, however, was deep respect and admiration. He was more of a father figure than my father.

"Jesus Christ, son, you still have it," he said.

Coach Samson was riding high on the back of a padded hitting dummy. Currently he was getting a sleigh ride across the football field, benefit of my churning legs and sweat. He had agreed to go over the basic fundamentals, because I had been out of football for seven years. And even a battle-scarred old war horse like myself could always use some basic training.

He blew a whistle and I stopped, dropping to my knees. We were alone on the varsity football field, although the school marching band was practicing in an adjacent field. School was still forty-five minutes from starting. The band, as far as I could tell, was one hundred percent African-American.

I might have been the last white to come through here.

Without his prodding, I got down into a three-point stance, and then lunged forward, hitting the padded dummy hard. Coach Samson held on, and I proceeded to push that goddamn thing up and down the field.

The coach instructed and advised as I went, reminding me to keep my head up and my back straight and to keep my legs churning.

I churned and churned all morning long, and I did not once think about Cindy, or that I had not heard from her in two days. And I did not once think about Derrick or the hitman, either.

Instead, I focused on football.

Sweet football.

A sport I had been born to play, a sport that had been taken from me. But I was determined to reclaim it—and my life.

Most of all, I tried to ignore the pain in my left leg.

That endless goddamn pounding.

42.

My father's offices are on the fifteenth floor of a major LA skyscraper. I regretted the decision to walk the stairs by the seventh floor. At the fifteenth floor, I found the nearest bathroom and splashed water on my face and neck, then headed through some heavy double doors. Above the door were the words: KNIGHT-HORSE INVESTIGATIONS.

A big, bald security guard was waiting behind a desk. He was about fifty. His uniform was neatly pressed. Probably a retired cop, or a retired colonel, a man who commanded respect. I immediately disliked him, partly because he worked for my father, partly because he was glaring at me.

"Can I help you?" he asked in a thick Boston accent.

"You're pretty big for a secretary," I said. "Do you also fetch the coffee?"

He frowned and his bushy eyebrows—the only hair on his head—formed one long bristly line. "I'm not a secretary."

"I'm sorry. Is that not politically correct these days? How about front desk technician? Is that better?"

He stared at me. The hairy caterpillar above his eyes twitched.

"Waddya want?"

"Cooper Knighthorse. He's the small guy with the creepy eyes."

"Yes, I'm aware of who he is."

"So you agree he has creepy eyes?"

"Do you have an appointment?"

"No, I thought I would surprise him. Dad always likes a good surprise. Take the time when I threw a brick through the car window when he was screwing a neighbor's wife in the back seat." I laughed heartily. "Let me tell you, good times for one and all."

"Dad?"

I nodded encouragingly.

"Mr. Knighthorse is your father?"

"I see you're no slouch. In fact, you might make a hell of a detective some day."

He ignored me. "Didn't know Coop had a son."

"Obviously, I'm his pride and joy," I said. "Now my father usually boffs his front desk engineers in the back room. Perhaps you were unaware of your full job description."

He made a move to stand up. "Don't push it, buddy."

I leaned over the desk. "But pushing it is what I do best."

He was a big guy, maybe a little soft around the middle. It would have been a hell of a fight if a voice hadn't come from my left. The voice belonged to my father. "He's okay, Reginald. He's a hardass, but he's okay."

"Your kid has a big mouth."

"Always has," said my father.

I walked around the desk and smiled at Reginald. "I'll take cream and sugar in my coffee."

DARK HORSE

43.

The entire fifteenth floor was occupied by my father's agency. His office was big, but not ornately so. There was a leather executive chair with brass nail trim behind a black lacquered desk. Piles of case folders everywhere, and from all indications, business was booming. No surprise there. He sat and motioned for me to do the same in one of his client chairs.

"Why you giving Reggie such a hard time?" my father asked.

"Just making friends and influencing people."

On his desk, angled in one corner and slightly pushed askew by an errant folder, was the picture of a blond woman and a little boy. I had no idea who they were. A different family, a different life. For all I knew the little boy could have been my half brother.

"Tell me about the pictures," I said.

He sat back in his chair and studied me silently. His gaze was unwavering. So was mine. Through the open window, in my peripheral vision, I saw a helicopter hover past, then dart away like a curious hummingbird. I tried not to let it distract me.

"What do you want to know?"

"I want to know why you gave them to me now."

"I only discovered them a few years ago."

"Why not give them to me then?"

"Because you were still working here as an apprentice."

"What does that matter?"

"You didn't know what the hell you were doing," he said.

I smiled, realizing what he was getting at. "You waited for me to become a detective."

"Actually, I waited for you to become a *good* detective."

"So you think I'm good?" I hated the fact

that this news pleased me.

"That's what I hear."

"You've been checking up on me."

He tilted his head toward me and shrugged. "I hear things."

"Meanwhile you just sat on these photos."

He shifted in his chair and looked away. "Yes."

"Tell me more about the photos."

"When I moved in with Candy," he nodded toward the blond on his desk, "I found them at the bottom of a box. I flipped through, the first time I had ever done so. To be honest, I don't know when they were developed or when I picked them up. Probably they were included with some other pictures, and got forgotten."

Something rose within me. Blood, anger, revulsion, hatred. "These were pictures of your murdered wife taken on the last day she was alive, the mother of your son, and they were forgotten in the bottom of a box?"

"Those were tough times. I really didn't know my head from a hole in the ground."

"Not a good analogy. Trust me you did just fine in that department. Remember, I saw first hand."

We were silent. I did my best to control my anger. On the wall behind him was a picture of a lighthouse. His paperweight was a lighthouse, as were his two bookends. Since when did my dad like lighthouses? There was so much I didn't know about the man, and so much I didn't care to know.

"They were fishing together, and one of them appears to have taken an interest in the two of you."

He sat back. "That's how I see it."

"It might have been more than an interest," I added.

"Perhaps. Could also be a coincidence."

I said, "Any idea who Blondie is in the picture?"

He shook his head sadly. "No."

"Do you remember him?"

"Vaguely."

"Were you aware that he had followed you back to the store?"

"No."

"Did you see him again at any other time?"

"No."

"Did you speak with him?"

"I think we did."

"Do you recall what was said?"

"No, I don't. I think I commented on the shark."

"Anything else?"

"Your mother made them laugh with the rabbit ears. They thought she was funny."

I digested this. "Since finding the pictures two years ago, have you done anything—*anything at all*—to follow up on your wife's murder?"

More shifting, as if the plush leather chair could possibly be uncomfortable. He motioned toward the files on his desk. "I've been busy lately, too busy, you know...."

"Let me finish for you, father. You were too busy making money to follow up on your wife's murder. Too busy solving other people's problems to worry about a woman you never truly loved."

He shrugged.

I got up and walked around the desk and looked down at him. I stood before him, breathing hard, blood pounding in my ears.

"Do what you've got to do," he said, "and get the hell out of here."

I backhanded him across the face. The force of the blow almost sent him over the arm of his chair. He regained his balance. A red welt was already forming on his cheek bone. Blood appeared in the corner of his mouth, then trickled out. He said nothing, did nothing, just watched me. His eyes were passionless and empty. No, not empty. There was something there, something deep within, something trying to climb up from the unfathomable depths of his cold soul, but then he blinked and it was gone.

44.

I was sitting next to a window drinking a large iced vanilla coffee when he appeared in the parking lot from behind a large truck. The day was hot, but he didn't seem to mind or notice his copious layers of clothing. In fact, he wasn't even sweating. Maybe he *was* God.

Once inside, he ordered a cup of coffee and sat opposite me, carefully prying the plastic lid off and blowing on his coffee. Finally, when appropriately cooled, he took a sip.

"So where do you go when you're not here

speaking with me?"

"Wherever I want."

"And where might that be?"

"It's not where you are, Jim, it's how you get there."

"Wow, that's nice. You should put that on a bumper sticker."

"Where do you think I got it?"

"Great, now God's quoting bumper stickers."

"It's an old truth, Jim."

"The journey and all that," I said.

"Yes, it's about the journey," he said, sipping quietly and watching me with his brownish eyes.

"And what happens once you get there?" I asked. "What happens once the journey is over?"

"That is for you to decide, my son. You can stay there, or you can start a new journey."

"A new journey?"

"Of course."

"Are we talking reincarnation here?" I asked.

"I don't know," said Jack. "Are we?"

"Does reincarnation exist?" I asked.

"The soul lives forever," said the bum in front of me as if he knew what the hell he was talking about. "But the soul can choose many forms."

"Okay, it's too early in the morning for this shit, Sorry I asked."

"Apology accepted. But there's a reason you asked, isn't there?"

There was, but I wasn't sure I wanted the answer. I put down my iced coffee and set it aside.

"So where's my mother now?" I asked. "You know, her spirit, or whatever?"

As I spoke, Jack inhaled the coffee deeply, pausing, taking the scent deep within, making it a part of him.

"She is wherever she wants to be," he said, exhaling.

"And where would that be?"

"For instance, she is with us now since we are talking about her."

"Oh really?"

"Yes."

"And is she sitting next to me?" I asked.

He didn't answer at first, although he gave me a gentle smile.

"She is in your heart, Jim. Be still, and feel her there."

I looked at the old man across from me. On second thought, he wasn't really that old. On third thought, I was hard pressed to gauge just how old he was, although he was certainly older than me. And then another thought occurred to me: My mother. I suddenly remembered a time when she and I had gone to the beach together in the city bus. She let me ditch school and had treated me like a prince that day.

My breath caught in my throat. Fuck, I missed her.

"She misses you, too," said Jack. "But she wants you to know that she is always with you." He paused, and that gentle smiled found his weathered face. "And that you will always be her little prince, even though you are a big son-of-bitch."

And all I could do was wipe my eyes and laugh.

Hi, mom.

45.

"Last time you were here, Knighthorse, my school was turned upside down. Please, no more bodies."

Vice Principal Williams's levity over the tragic suicide of her football coach was a tad alarming, but I let it slide without comment. She had come to the door to shake my hand. Today she was dressed in a white pant suit and a white blouse that was see-through enough to ignite the imagination of any hormone-enraged teenaged boy. And to ignite the imagination of at least one hormone-enraged detective.

"Um, nice blouse," I said.

"Thank you," she said. She looked down at it. "Or are you just saying that because you can see the outline of my bra?"

"Which qualifies it as a nice blouse."

She settled into her chair behind her desk. I sat before her. Her gaze did not waver from mine. "I am a married woman."

I pointed to the rock on her hand. "Not a hard fact to overlook, even for one as highly trained as I."

"What makes you so highly trained?"

"I apprenticed for two years with my father. And he is the best."

"You say that almost grudgingly."

"My father and I have never been close. You could say he was unsupportive in my earlier sporting endeavors."

"You hold that against him?"

"Yes."

She studied me some more, and we held each other's gaze for a heartbeat or two. She inhaled and her chest inflated and the lacy bra pushed out. It was a calculated move.

"Currently my husband and I are separated."

"I see."

"What is your situation, Mr. Knighthorse?"

I hesitated. I did not know my situation.

Cindy had not called me for two days. As far as I knew she was gone.

"I am in a similar situation," I said.

"Perhaps we can entertain each other in the meantime."

"Entertaining is good."

"How about dinner this weekend?" she asked.

I thought about it. It was getting old drinking alone.

"Mrs. Williams—"

"Please, Dana."

"Dana, this weekend would be...fine."

She smiled, relaxed and sat back. She had the attitude of a closed deal. "Now what can I do for you?"

"Where can I find the school band director?"

"Bryan Dawson?"

"If that's the band director."

Her fingers drummed the arm of her chair.

"Is there a problem, Dana?" I asked.

She turned in her swivel chair and gazed out her considerable window into the empty quad. I continued to watch her, intrigued by her response.

"Why do you wish to speak to him?"

"Amanda quit the school band unexpectedly. I want to find out why."

"Seems a reach for your investigation."

"My job is to reach. Luckily I have a long arm."

"You can find him here in the mornings. Room one oh seven, around six a.m. Band practice starts at zero period, six forty-five a.m."

"Is there something I should know about him?" I asked.

"What do you mean?"

"Look, I'm a good detective. Perhaps not as good as my pop, but the next best thing. If there's something going on with your band director, I'm going to find out about it. But you and I can cut a deal now, and if you make things easy on me, perhaps I will agree to keep things quiet."

"*Perhaps*?"

"Perhaps is the best I can offer."

"*Perhaps* is not good enough."

"Then I will find the truth on my own, and there is no deal."

She sat back and gazed at me from over steepled fingers. "You are a hard sonofabitch."

"You have no idea."

"I just want myself and the school left out of it."

"I can probably swing that," I said.

"*Probably*?"

"Best I can offer right now."

She got up and shut her door, then sat back

down and faced me. She didn't look me in the eye. Instead she busied herself by adjusting her desk calendar this way and that. She only risked glancing up at me occasionally. Even then she seemed to only focus on my unnaturally broad shoulders. Who could blame her, really?

"Now, there have been some, ah, alleged indiscretions between Mr. Dawson and a couple of his students in the past."

"Have the allegations been confirmed?"

"No."

"Was Amanda Peterson one of those who allegedly had an indiscretion?"

"Yes."

"What did these indiscretions involve?"

"Sexual advances."

"Has anyone looked into the allegations?"

"I did."

"And what did you discover?"

"He denied everything and there was no proof, and now one of the girls is dead."

"And the other?"

"Lives in Washington state."

"Do you have her address?"

She looked at me blankly. Then turned to her filing cabinet behind her, opened it, and busied herself for the next minute or two thumbing through files. She removed one and brought it to her desk. There she copied some information down on a sticky pad, then passed it over to me. There was a name on it, Donna Trigger, along with a phone number.

Dana sat back. "You are very thorough."

"No stone unturned."

"Are you just as thorough in the bedroom?"

"You'll just have to use your imagination."

She smiled, and her cheeks turned a little red.

"Oh, I have."

46.

I figure if I'm going to haul my ass out to Huntington High by six a.m., then I was going to reward myself with some Krispy Kremes.

Which I did, along with two containers of chocolate milk. I don't drink coffee, and since I'm still looking to add some weight, whole chocolate milk has the kind of calories I'm looking for.

It was cool enough for the heater, and since I didn't want to waste all my precious calories shivering, I went ahead and cranked it up. With the ocean to my right, I drove languidly south along Pacific Coast Highway. I was not in a hurry and I had my donuts to keep me company. The ocean was slate gray and choppy this morning, but that did not stop the handful of faithful surfers, who dotted the breakers like so much flotsam.

I turned up a street called Mariner, which, coincidentally, just happened to be Huntington High's mascot, and neatly finished the last of the Krispy Kremes, slugging it down with the remainder of the chocolate milk. I pulled into the visitor parking spot. My gun had traveled on the seat next to me; these days I kept it particularly handy.

I licked my fingers clean before grabbing the gun and shoving it in my shoulder holster. I just hate sticky gun handles.

***

I was waiting outside room 107 when I heard footsteps coming from the adjoining hall-way.

Instinctively I reached inside my jacket and rested my hand on the handle of the Browning. A man appeared from around the corner. He was young-looking and in his early thirties, thick black hair and a nice build. His face was narrow and clean-shaven. He was a handsome guy; worse, he knew it.

When he saw me, he paused in mid-step.

"Bryan Dawson?" I asked.

He made an effort to smile broadly. It was a good smile, the kind that would melt any impressionable high schooler. However, I was not an impressionable high schooler.

"You are the detective," he said, brushing past me, knocking a shoulder into mine. It was a calculated shoulder strike, but I didn't move. He careened briefly off-balance and only recovered by grabbing the door handle.

"Pardon you," I said. "Are you okay?"

"Oh, yes, sorry. A little clumsy this early in the morning."

He had known of me, which I found interesting. Someone had hired the thug, too; someone who had known of me as well.

"Don't worry about it. I'm just glad your shoulder is okay," I said jovially. "How do you know me?"

"Someone pointed you out the other day when the police arrived for Coach Castleton. Weren't you the one who found him?"

"Yes."

"Must have been awful," he said. "Seeing his brains and shit all over the place."

His gaze was unwavering and challenging. I

didn't like him. He was cocky, loud, and too sure of himself.

"It was more awful that he found it necessary to end his life. The murder of Amanda Peterson has had significant repercussions. Not to mention an innocent boy is in jail for the crime."

"The police don't seem to think he's so innocent. For them it's an open and shut case."

"Luckily for Derrick, I don't think it's so open and shut."

"Which means what? You're only a private dick."

"Means I'm going to find the killer."

"So what can I do for you?"

"May I come in?"

"No."

"Did you have a relationship with Amanda?"

"I was her band director."

"Did you have a relationship with her outside of school?"

"Of course not."

"Where were you on the night of Amanda Peterson's murder?"

"I have nothing left to say to you."

"Of course you don't."

And he promptly shut the door in my face.

Jim Knighthorse, master interrogator.

47.

It was late and we were at a restaurant called Waters in the city of Irvine. Coincidentally, a small, foul-smelling, man-made lake sat next to the restaurant. I wondered what came first: The lake or the restaurant?

Vice Principal Dana Williams had pushed hard for this meeting, so I agreed to meet her here. I sensed she liked me. I also sensed she was a very lonely woman. So why had I agreed? I didn't know entirely. She was loosely connected to my case, so I could always justify the meeting in that way. I was also lonely myself. Very lonely. Perhaps we were just two lost souls meeting in the night, at a pretentiously named restaurant.

"Do you talk to your ex-girlfriend much?" asked Mrs. Williams. She emphasized the *ex* part a little too much.

"She's not my ex. We're just taking a break from all the action."

"What sort of action?" she asked.

"Nevermind," I said. I didn't feel like talking about it, especially someone who was all for my break up with Cindy. Anyone who was all for my break up with Cindy was no friend of mine.

"Do you always speak in football jargon?" she asked.

We were seated outside, on the wide, wooden deck that wrapped around the entire restaurant. We had a great view of the fake lake. A duck floated nearby. It could have been fake, too, but I doubted it.

"Yes," I said simply.

"I see," she said. She toyed with the red straw sticking out of her margarita. If my lack of enthusiasm for our meeting was making her uncomfortable, she didn't show it. I sensed that she saw me as a challenge. "Do you think I'm pretty?" she asked suddenly.

Admittedly, the question caught me off-guard. I looked at her from across the table. She was looking ravishing, to say the least. A tight blouse that showed way too much of her chest. Make-up that seemed expertly applied. Hair perfectly framing her pretty face.

"Yeah," I said. I wasn't in the mood to dance around the subject.

She beamed, pleased.

Our food arrived. Clams for her. A burger for me. I ate the fries first. She watched me eat. She was about to ask me something, probably something about Cindy, when I cut her off. Enough of the bullshit.

"So how long have you been separated?" I asked.

She shrugged, sipped her drink. "I don't know."

"You don't know?"

She leveled her stare at me and I was reminded again that she was very much the vice principal of discipline at Huntington High. When she spoke, she lowered her voice ominously. "I don't remember, *exactly*. A few years I suppose. Is that okay?"

"Hey, I'm okay if you're okay," I said, and very much wanted to get the hell out of here. Mrs. Williams's apparent ability to go from flirtatious to bitch was alarming at best.

We ate our food in silence. Actually, I ate and she toyed. I wondered what the clams thought about being killed only to be toyed with.

Probably be pissed off.

"Do you think Derrick killed Amanda?" I asked suddenly. Hey, might as well get some work done. In the least, I could write the dinner off for tax purposes.

"Yes," she said immediately.

"Why?"

"He had motive and he had the murder weapon."

"Damning evidence," I said. "Except that all indications seem to point that he was truly in love with Amanda."

"Which would make his jealousy all the more unpredictable," she said. "Wouldn't it?"

I shrugged. I didn't like answering leading questions.

We continued to eat. Just beyond, the duck floated unmovingly. I was now certain it was fake. Or asleep.

While we ate, I could sense Mrs. Williams watching me. Her watching me made me uncomfortable in a way I couldn't quite put my finger on. Perhaps I sensed in her an unpredictability. She reminded me of my father in that way. Happy one moment, a real piece of work the next.

And for perhaps the hundredth time that evening, I wished with all my heart that Cindy was sitting across from me. I missed her laugh, her smile, her scent. Her everything.

When the bill came, I quickly paid it and we left. As we exited the restaurant, Mrs. Williams looped her arm through mine. I think I shuddered a little.

I walked her to her car, where we stood awkwardly for a few moments. I wanted to leave but she wouldn't release my arm. Above, the tiny sliver of moon reflected the hollow feeling inside me.

"I had a great time tonight," she said.

Her words took me by surprise. What date had she been on? I had been miserable.

"We should do it again sometime," she added.

I nodded dumbly and just wanted to leave. Finally she released my arm and surprised me again by planting a big, wet kiss on my lips. She pulled away and grinned warmly, then got in her massive SUV and drove off.

I stood there in the parking lot, watching her go.

I wanted to run to Cindy.

But I didn't. Instead, on the way home, I bought a case of beer and drank the night away.

48.

I went on a seven mile jog the next morning. I kept an easy pace, and my leg only hurt a little, which was encouraging. I showered and shaved at home, then headed for the office, where I kept my office door locked and the Browning on the desk next to me.

I called Donna Trigger. A girl answered and told me that Donna had classes this morning but I could try later in the afternoon. I said I would, she said cool, popped a bubble and hung up.

Next I called Sanchez on his cell and asked

him to run Bryan Dawson's name through his data base and see what turned up. He said no problem and that if it weren't for me he wouldn't have shit to do, nevermind his caseload of homicides to solve. I hung up on him in mid-rant.

I sat back in my chair and realized I had no real clues or suspects, other than two lecherous men with a fondness for young girls. This was so depressing that I felt it necessary to take a nap. I usually don't need much convincing when it comes to naps.

***

The phone woke me. It was just before noon.

"Hi," said a soft voice. My heart lurched. It was Cindy.

"Hello."

"Can I see you?"

"Sure."

"I'll be there in twenty minutes."

I hung up and sat at my desk for a minute or two until I realized I was holding my breath. I let it out slowly. Within the next few minutes the course of my life would be set. Amazingly, it was out of my hands, and in Cindy's alone.

***

I stood off to the side of my window, look-ing down onto Beach Blvd, the blinds partly open. Hauling ass down the street and turning dangerously in front of a white pickup, Cindy arrived in her silver Lexus. I could hear the pickup's angry horn from here.

And trailing behind Cindy was a blue Tau-rus. Not normally a big deal, granted, but sitting in the driver's seat was my friend the hitman. He continued on past my building and made a left and disappeared.

He made two mistakes: the first was that I made his plate. The second was that he had in-volved Cindy.

My phone rang. I grabbed it.

"You're girlfriend's cute. Back off, or she's dead." The line went dead.

I immediately called Sanchez and got his voice mail. I left the plate number for him to run. Now I was going to owe Sanchez another dinner. So what else was new?

Next I unlocked the door and paced before my couch, trying like hell to get the killer out of my mind and focus on Cindy. To focus on *us*.

Moving along the cement walkway, heels clicking rapidly along, I could hear Cindy coming.

My hands were sweating; my shoulders were knotted. I resented her for putting me through this. We had been serious for eight years. She knew the dangers inherent to my profession, but she also knew that I could handle them. The only new twist was my interest in resuming my football career; well, and the drinking.

The door to my office opened, and she stood there holding a beautiful bouquet of wildflowers. She came in and set the flowers down on the desk, then threw her arms around me. Her lips found mine and we kissed like lost lovers, which, for a few days, we were. We fumbled our way to the couch, and there we made up for lost time.

And the direction of my life became clear again.

Damn clear.

49.

Nestled between a Rite Aide and a laundromat was a little Italian place that I liked, called Frazzi's. Cindy and I were heading there now for lunch, holding hands. The mid-day sun shone straight down on us, but lacked any real heat, just a bright ornament hanging in the sky.

"So why is Italian your favorite food?" asked Cindy. I sensed she was feeling happy. The weather was nice, and we had just made love, and she wanted to keep things light and fun, at least for the moment. We still hadn't talked about the heavy stuff, which was fine by me.

"I've discovered in the course of my considerable dining experience and extensive travels that a food joint has to work pretty damn hard to screw up Italian food. It's usually a sure bet."

"I've screwed it up before," she said.

"Actually, we screwed it up together," I said.

"Which is why we no longer cook."

"And why we eat out."

"Except for you and your damn cereal and PB&Js."

"Cereal and PB&J's are my staple. They keep me alive."

"I know. I think it's cute."

Frazzi's was a narrow restaurant with checkered table cloths and red vinyl seats. We found a booth in the back and sat ourselves. By now Cindy knows to allow me to have the best view of the restaurant, where I keep my eyes on the front door, the butt of my gun loose and free. There wasn't much for Cindy to look at other than me. Lucky girl.

The waitress came by and we ordered two Cokes.

"So can I say a few things?" asked Cindy.

"Of course." Here it comes.

"Your drinking worries me. Actually, it's not

the fact that you occasionally get drunk, it's that you feel you need to drink secretly."

"Well, it's not a pretty sight."

"How long have you been getting drunk?"

I shrugged. "Off and on since I broke my leg."

"The broken leg was the catalyst?"

"Yes."

"And nothing else?"

I reached out and took her hand from across the table. She needed to be reassured. I looked at her steadily in the eye. "It's the only reason."

"Nothing about me?"

"No."

"Can I ask you a favor?"

"Yes," I said.

"Will you try to stop for me? I'm not asking you to give up drinking altogether, but I'm asking you to stop getting drunk whenever we are away from each other, to stop destroying your liver, to stop feeling so goddamn sorry for yourself."

"I might need help."

"I'll help you."

Our drinks came, along with some fresh bread and oil.

"The usual, Jim?" asked Mama Lucco. She was Italian and in her mid-forties. I'd been coming here for four years, ever since I set up my agency down the street.

"Make that two," I said.

When Mama Lucco had moved off, Cindy asked, "What's the usual?"

"Lasagna, of course."

"I should have known."

"So what else is on your mind?"

She took a sip from her Coke, and then tore a piece of bread off, dipped it in oil and gave it to me. I took it, and she repeated the process for herself.

When she was ready, she said, "I've been feeling sorry for myself, too, admittedly. I asked myself why couldn't I have a boyfriend who has a normal job, a job in which his life isn't threatened by a hired killer, a job that didn't require you to deal with the dregs of society."

She paused. I waited.

"But then I realized that you are so goddamn good at what you do, and someone has to set things right in this fucked up world. And if you are willing to do it, then the least I can do is stand by your side, and give you my support."

I digested this, then asked, "What about football?"

"I don't know what to make of this football business. We'll cross that bridge when we get there."

"Fair enough."

"And I've come to the conclusion that if I go back to you now, I will forever accept you, just the way you are, and deal with whatever comes our way, together. I had a taste of life without you this week, and it was horrible. Just horrible." She paused and took my hand, and looked me in the eye. "Will you take me back?"

"Yes," I said.

She kissed my knuckles. "You've got me forever, Jim Knighthorse. Or for as long as you can stand me."

50.

Later, with Cindy teaching an afternoon class, and me wondering how I was going to stay off the booze, Sanchez called.

"I got an address on that plate."

"Swell."

"You say it was an older model *blue* Taurus?"

"Uh huh."

"How about a *green* '89 Taurus?"

"Green, blue, same difference."

"Christ, Knighthorse. Can't you tell the difference?"

"No," I said. "Greens and blues are tough."

"That could be the difference in apprehending a felon."

"We all have our handicaps," I said. "Mine is coloration. Yours is unattractiveness."

"Fuck you," he said, chuckling.

"Perhaps if you were better looking."

"So what are you going to do?"

"Convince the killer to stay away."

Sanchez was silent. "You're going to kill him," he finally said. It wasn't a question.

"No other way to convince a hitman to stay away."

"You need help?"

"Wouldn't that be against the law?"

"Yes."

"No, thank you. He made it personal. Be better if you stayed out of it, in case something goes wrong." I paused. "I owe you."

"Fucking eh, you do. You can start with dinner tonight."

He gave me the name and address, and hung up. Johnny Bright. I stared at the name for some time.

He should have left Cindy out of it. Would have been healthier for him.

***

Next I called Washington state, and this time got hold of Donna Trigger.

"Who's this?" she asked. Her voice was soft.

"My name is Jim Knighthorse, I'm a private detective down in Huntington Beach. I'm following up on the murder of Amanda Peterson."

There was silence. Not even a hiss of a connection. "What can I do for you, Mr. Knighthorse?"

"Can I ask you about Bryan Dawson?"

Another pause. "What would you like to know?"

"What was your relationship with Mr. Dawson?"

"He was my band director," she said evenly. "And my lover." She caught me admittedly by surprise. But I am a professional, and just as I opened my mouth for the next question, she continued: "And, in the end, my stalker."

"Could you elaborate?"

"On what?"

"On everything," I said.

***

She did, and when we hung up I had a much clearer picture of Bryan Dawson. And I had no reason to doubt her.

Dawson had approached her during her junior year, and she had been flattered because she had always considered him cute. All of the girls did. It began after band camp when he offered to give her a ride home. One thing led to another and they didn't make it home and she had been honored that he had chosen *her* out of all the girls. She was seventeen and had been a virgin. She saw him secretly during the next year, but he became possessive and physical and she ended the relationship. He was relentless in his pursuit to win her back. Soon he was following her home, standing outside her windows, calling her repeatedly. And when she began dating someone else, a senior at their school, that someone was brutally attacked one night, leaving the kid with a fractured skull and permanent semi-blindness.

But the stalking had abruptly ended when he found a new girl.

A replacement.

Amanda Peterson.

51.

Sanchez and I were across the street from my pad, upstairs at the Huntington Beach Brew Pub.

"Why am I always coming out to O.C. to meet you?" he asked.

"Because I'm worth it," I said. "What's Danielle doing tonight?"

"She's taking a class. Going back to school to get a degree in finance. She's hit a ceiling at work, needs the degree."

"It's about time you let her have a life you

chauvinistic Latino pig."

"Hey, I'm only half Latino."

We were both drinking the blond house draft, a light, sweet beer.

Sanchez said, "Why is it the blond beer is the lighter beer, and the darker beer gets you drunk faster? Thought blonds have more fun."

"How long you been thinking that one up?"

"Just came to me. I am, after all, a UCLA-educated Latino."

Our food came. And lots of it. I had ordered from the appetizer menu, running my forefinger straight down the list and rattling off anything that sounded good. And it all sounded good. Now, plates of nachos, chicken wings, calamari, southwestern eggrolls and even an artichoke were arriving steadily at our table.

"Someone in the kitchen must like you," said Sanchez, "because they gave you a green flower."

"It's called an artichoke, you oaf."

"Well, your arteries are going to be choking after you eat all that shit."

Despite myself, I laughed.

"What can I say?" Sanchez said. "I'm on a roll. Can I have any of that shit?"

"Get your own food."

"Can't; you cleaned out the kitchen."

We drank from our beer. The Lakers were

playing the Jazz. Shaq was unloading on them.

"So I've got news on Pencil Dick."

"Who's Pencil Dick?"

"Your teacher friend, Bryan Dawson. Anyone poking high school students is called a pencil dick."

"I see; what's the news?"

Sanchez leaned forward on his elbows. "Pencil Dick was involved in another murder up north. In a city called Half Moon Bay."

"So tell me."

"A student of his, a band student, disappeared. They found her floating in the San Francisco bay. Pencil Dick was a suspect, but they couldn't pin anything on him. He quit his job and came down here."

"Well, then, what do you think we should do?" I asked.

"We tail him. With Amanda gone, he might be looking for new blood."

J.R. RAIN

52.

I found the allegedly green Taurus parked in front of a small woodframe house in Santa Ana. It was 9:00 p.m., and the Taurus still looked blue to me.

Santa Ana is mostly Hispanic and its residents are perhaps the poorest in Orange County. In fact, downtown Santa Ana looks as if it had been lifted whole from Mexico City.

Johnny Bright, as a Caucasian, would stick out in Santa Ana like a sore white thumb.

But one question remained: was Johnny

Bright the same guy who took a potshot at my ear? The vehicle could have belonged to a friend. In that case I would follow the friend. Either way, with a paid killer on my ass, I preferred to be proactive in my involvement with him.

I waited in my car around a corner, with a clear view of Bright's front porch. My own vehicle had nicely tinted windows, and from behind them I watched the house through lightweight high-powered binoculars. I didn't have many tools of the trade, but this was one of them.

I was listening to Will Durant's *Story of Philosophy* on tape. The 5 Freeway arched above the housing tract. Freeway noises, especially the rumble of a Harley, cut through the drone of the tape. I was on my third tape, marching on through Voltaire and the French Enlightenment, when four gang members stopped by the Mustang and looked it over, not realizing I was inside. I rolled down my window and reached under my seat and pulled out a fake police badge.

Another one of my tools....

"Can I help you gentlemen?" I said, flashing the badge.

The first one, a skinny kid with a black bandana tied around his head, shot his hands up as if I had pointed a gun at him. When he spoke he had a long, drawling Hispanic accent, punctuated by jerky hand movements.

"Don't shoot me, officer, I didn't mean to look at your killer set of wheels."

"You can look but don't touch."

"Waddya doin' here?" asked the kid, their obvious leader.

"Watching you boys."

"Are you gay, too?"

His buddies slapped each other high fives.

Behind them there was movement in Bright's house, but I couldn't see because the gang members were in my way. I heard a screen door swing open and slap shut.

"Beat it," I said.

The three of them waited for their leader. The leader squinted at me and seemed to recognize me. I get this kind of partial recognition a lot. Probably because at one point in their lives they had seen me on their TV screens, or in their newspapers, or sports magazines. But this kid was young, perhaps too young to know of me. But you never knew.

He jerked his head. "Let's roll," he told the others.

They sauntered off. One called me a pig. They would be potential witnesses; that is, if the police tried very hard to investigate the murder.

Murder?

Yeah, someone's going to die tonight.

Across the street, Fuck Nut, with his slicked-back graying hair visible from even here, opened the door to his Taurus and got in.

53.

We drove through Santa Ana. I tailed him using tricks gleaned from my father. Once, at a red light, I even turned into a liquor store parking lot. When the light turned green again, I pulled out of the parking lot and continued tailing him.

At least I was amusing myself.

He pulled into a Taco Bell, and I waited across the street. He went through the drive-thru, and when he exited I followed him back to his house.

Across the street, I waited for him to finish his tacos, since it was his last meal. As I waited, I listened to the beating of my heart, filling the silence now that the book on tape had been turned off. The thudding filled my ears, and I focused on that rather than what was about to come. What had to come. I didn't think of myself as a killer, but sometimes you had to do what you had to do. I needed this guy off my ass and away from Cindy.

When twenty minutes had passed, I stepped out of my car, crossed the street and walked up his front porch. The porch was made of cement, and my footfalls made no sound.

I stood before the door, aimed for the area under the doorknob, lifted my foot and smashed it open. Wood splintered. The door swung open on one hinge, and I kicked it the rest of the way open.

"What the fuck?" came a startled voice from inside.

Johnny Bright, a.k.a. Fuck Nut, was now dressed in a wife beater and blue boxers. On the coffee table before him was a porn magazine. There were little boys on the cover. He had dropped his soft taco in his alarm, and had just wrapped his fingers around the handle of his own 9mm.

Standing in the doorway, I shot him four

times in the chest.

When I was about three miles away, in a city called Fountain Valley, I pulled over to the side of the road and threw up my breakfast, lunch and dinner.

And I kept throwing up....

J.R. RAIN

54.

He was waiting for me at the back of McDonald's. I sat down without ordering. I was still feeling sick to my stomach, and the thought of a greasy McGriddle did little to alleviate the queasiness.

I didn't look him in the eye, although I could feel his on me. Today, he was smelling especially ripe, as if he had slept in a dumpster. Hell, as if he *was* a dumpster.

A few minutes of this and I finally risked looking up. He was smiling at me kindly, and the love and warmth in his eyes was almost unbearable.

"I'm sorry," I said.

"What are you sorry for?" he asked.

"If you are God, you know."

We were silent some more. I didn't feel like playing his head games today. If he was God, then let him take the next step. If not, then I was content to sit across from him until the smell of frying bacon made me hurl. Which might be sooner rather than later.

"He was a very troubled man," said Jack.

"Yes, he was,"

"He made many poor choices."

I took in some air. The queasiness seemed to intensify as I relived Fuck Nut's last moments.

"Perhaps his poorest choice was threatening Cindy," said Jack.

I had never once mentioned Cindy's name to the man sitting across from me. The fact that he knew who she was should have amazed me, but in my current state of disarray, it was mostly lost on me.

"A very poor choice," I said.

"And you were forced to take action to protect her."

"Yes."

"So what are you sorry for?"

"For killing him."

"He wanted to die, Jim. He knew this day was coming. He was miserable and lonely and hated every day that he was alive."

I said nothing. I could not speak. His words did, however, ease some of the queasiness. I sat a little straighter even as I felt a little better.

"Is he going to hell?" I asked.

"He is in a place you do not want to be."

We'd had this discussion before and I didn't feel like getting into it now. There was no heaven or hell, but only worlds of our own creations. There was no punishment in the after-life, only reflection and recreation. Blah blah blah. New age mumbo-jumbo. I didn't want to hear it. I had killed a man and that was my reality.

"He hurt a lot of kids, too," I said.

"Yes."

"Hey, I've got a fucking question for you, Jack...God, or whoever the fuck you are. Why the fuck did you allow him to hurt innocent kids? There you go. Answer that question. I'm sure there's a million mothers out there who've lost innocent children who'd just love an answer to that one. Oh, wait, never mind. You're just a bum and I'm a fucking idiot for coming in to a fucking McDonald's and entertaining the idea that you might be something more than just street trash." I stopped, took a deep breath.

"You done?" asked Jack.

I nodded, sitting back, my heart yammering in my chest.

"Nobody dies without the spirit's consent," said Jack.

"So a child who's kidnapped, raped and buried alive gives such a consent."

"Yes."

"But they're a fucking child, Jack. How the fuck could a child make that kind of a decision?"

"The decision was made long ago."

"Long ago? You mean in a place where time suddenly *does* exist?"

He ignored my sarcasm.

"Prior to taking on the body, the soul made an agreement with another soul—"

I cut him off; this was just pissing me off.

"An agreement to allow themselves to be raped and killed? How very generous of the soul."

Jack looked at me for a long moment.

"Yes," he said. "Very generous."

"And that's supposed to comfort a grieving mother? A mother who, say, just lost her child to a sick-ass motherfucker?"

"Such a death serves many purposes, Jim. There is a ripple effect that will touch many, many lives for generations to come."

"Fine. Many lives are touched. It's a noble act of sacrifice. But it's the thought of their child suffering that drives parents mad with grief. The fact that their baby *suffered* at the hands of an animal."

Jack said nothing, although he did finally sip his coffee. Glad to see he still had his taste for coffee.

Finally, he said, "You might be pleased to know that a spirit may leave the body whenever it wants."

"A child could leave its body?"

"Yes."

"And not suffer?"

Jack looked at me and smiled very deeply and kindly, and I saw, for the first time ever, that there were tears in his eyes.

"And not suffer," he said.

"You promise?"

"I promise."

55.

Two days later I was in San Diego, about an hour and a half south from Huntington Beach.

It was 10:00 a.m. sharp and I was sitting alone in a leather sofa in an ornate office overlooking the lush playing field at Qualcomm Stadium. The field, as viewed through the massive window, was empty.

The office was covered with photographs of past personnel and players. I recognized almost all of them, since football was my life. Not to mention, I had taken a particularly keen interest in the San Diego Chargers since their last offer.

I was dressed to the nines in khakis and cordovan loafers and a blue silk shirt that accentuated my blue eyes. At least that's what I'm told.

A door opened and a little bald man with gold rimmed glasses came in. He saw me, smiled brightly, and moved over to me with surprising speed. Of course, it shouldn't be too surprising, Aaron Larkin had been free safety for the Chargers for most of his career in the seventies. In the seventies, he had not been bald.

"My God, Knighthorse, you are a big boy," he said, pumping my hand.

"Oh, really? I hadn't noticed."

He laughed and gestured for me to sit. He moved behind his black lacquer desk and took a seat. Larkin leaned forward eagerly and laced his fingers together before him. His fingers were thick and gnarled and some seemed particularly crooked, not too surprising after a full career in football. Between high school, college and the pros, fingers were bound to get broken.

"We are very excited to hear from you," Aaron Larkin began.

"Excitement is good. I am happy to be here."

"Well, we had given up on you. Such a tragedy about your leg. But my God you have kept yourself fit. And we need someone like you badly. Hell, who doesn't need a fullback nowadays?"

"Outside of football, few people."

He laughed. "We want to give you a private workout in two weeks. If we like what we see we'll invite you to training camp. We are honored that you're here, Knighthorse. My God you were an unholy terror on the playing field. Your services could be very, very valuable to us. So how is the leg?" he asked, and his voice was filled with genuine concern, and for that I liked the guy immensely.

"It has healed completely." I lied. It hurt like a motherfucker.

"An utter miracle. I watched you coming down the hall. There's no limp to speak of."

The hallways had been empty. He must have been watching me on some closed circuit TV. A sort of high tech surveillance to monitor my gait.

"Well, I'm a hell of a specimen."

"Around here, they all are."

We set a date for my mini-workout, and when I left his office, I waved to the little camera situated in the upper corner of the hallway.

56.

"Where the hell is he?" asked Sanchez.

I shrugged.

"Did you just shrug?" he asked. "Because it's too dark to tell. I mean there's a hundred reasons why I'm one of the best homicide detectives in LAPD, but seeing in the dark ain't one of them."

"Neither is using proper English."

"Hell you're lucky I'm using any English at all, being of Latino descent, and this being Southern California."

"This is America, you know."

"Unfortunately there ain't no such thing as speaking *American*."

"Too bad."

"And last time I checked we ain't in England, so fuck English."

We were waiting outside of Huntington High in my Mustang. It was past 7:00 p.m., and Bryan Dawson, or Pencil Dick, was still in his office. We had been waiting here for the past four hours. Students were long gone, including most of the faculty. We had watched the sun set over the Pacific.

"I'm hungry," said Sanchez.

"There's a Wendy's around the corner. Why don't you go get us something to eat."

"Why don't you give me the fucking money to go get us something to eat."

"When was the last time you paid for anything?" I asked.

"The last time you helped me solve a case."

I gave him the cash. Sanchez left, and the mere thought of a burger and fries made my stomach start to growl. We had been following Pencil Dick for four straight days. So far there was no evidence of any extracurricular activities on the part of the band director, other than his fondness for frozen yogurt.

Sanchez came back with a massive grease-stained bag of food. We ate silently and quickly, drinking from two plastic buckets that were passed off as jumbo drinks. And when we were finished, when the eating noises finally stopped altogether, when the debris had been collected back into the bags, I saw a familiar sight.

Coming down through a side hall, turning into the faculty parking lot, was a handsome man with dark hair. He was carrying a briefcase, and looked far too important to be just a band director. Or at least that was the impression he presented. He got into a red Jetta.

"Let's roll," I said.

57.

Bryan Dawson lived in a condo about a mile from the beach. We were currently heading in the opposite direction.

"He's not heading home," said Sanchez.

"Astute," I said.

I was three cars behind the Huntington band director, sometimes drifting back to four or five. To date, he had made no indication that he knew he was being followed.

"You're following too close."

"No, I'm not."

"He's going to make us."

"He's not going to make us," I said. "And I'm the one who taught you how to tail."

"But I'm the one who got all the tail."

"So you say."

We were heading deeper into Huntington Beach. In fact, we were just a few blocks from my office.

"Know someone works around here," said Sanchez. "Thinks he's a detective."

The Jetta suddenly turned into an empty bank parking lot. I pulled to the side of the road and killed the headlights, giving us a good view of Pencil Dick. From the shadows, a lithe figured stepped away from the building and into Dawson's car. The Jetta swung around, exited the parking lot and was soon heading back our way. Sanchez and I both ducked.

"You realize that we look like fools," said Sanchez as the car sped past us. "The windows are tinted. They can't see us."

"They especially can't see you," I said.

"Is that a comment on my darkish skin?"

"Your *dark* skin."

"I'm proud of my dark skin."

"Good for you," I said, peeking up and looking in my rearview mirror. Dawson was heading south, probably home. I flicked on the lights. "And away we go."

58.

I followed four car lengths behind the Jetta. Judging by Dawson's preoccupation with his newly acquired passenger, I probably could have followed directly behind him with my brights on, with little fear of being made.

"She just disappeared," said Sanchez.

"In his lap," I said.

"You think she's inspecting the quality of his zipper?"

"She's inspecting something."

The Jetta swerved slightly to the right. Dawson over-compensated and swerved to the left. He finally regained some control, although he now drove more toward the right side of the lane and even on the line itself.

"Seems distracted," said Sanchez.

"Yep."

"How old do you think she is?"

"No way of telling yet," I said.

"In the least, gonna nail him for statutory rape."

"Got the camera?"

Sanchez reached around and grabbed a nifty piece of equipment. It was a high resolution camcorder with night vision capabilities.

"So you know how to work this thing?" he asked.

"No idea. But we should figure it out fairly quickly."

The Jetta braked and made a right into a massive condo complex. I pulled immediately into a maintenance parking spot near the trash dumpster.

"Okay," Sanchez said, "I've got it rolling."

"Zoom in on the car."

I heard the whir of the zoom feature, and watched the lens stretch out like a probing eye. A green light feature indicated that the night vision capability was currently being used.

"Keep it steady," I said.

"That's what your mom told me back in high school."

"I didn't know you back in high school. Plus, my mom was killed when I was ten."

He pulled away from the camera. "No shit? How was she killed?"

"I don't want to talk about it."

He shrugged, lifted the camera back up to his eye. "Fine."

I said, "Here they come."

"Nice choice of words."

The girl emerged from her position in his lap. We both hunched down. The doors opened. I peeked through the steering wheel. Although the windshield was tinted, it was not as dark as the door glass. Someone looking hard enough could still spot us.

"You need to get a van. This is bullshit."

"When you talk the camera moves. So don't."

They headed our way, laughing and holding hands. Dawson's shirt was untucked. They continued toward us. Sanchez turned in his seat and followed them. As if on cue, Dawson stopped next to Sanchez's door, turned the girl around, planted a big kiss on her lips, and felt her up.

"You getting this?" I whispered.

"Oh, yeah."

"How old do you think she is?" I asked.

They continued up a flight of stairs and disappeared. Sanchez pulled the camera away from his eye.

"Too young."

I said, "Goodbye, Pencil Dick."

59.

I was in my office, feet up on my desk, fingers laced behind my head, a classic detective pose. Of course I had just finished doing two hundred military push ups. Let's see Colombo do that.

When the burn in my arms and chest had resided, I did some tricep dips along the edge of my desk. I've been doing these tricep dips every day since I was fifteen. I could do them all day long. I was at two hundred and seventy-one when my fax machine turned on. I cranked out another twenty-nine, because I like things neat and tidy, finishing in a flourish just as the fax machine stopped spitting out its image.

The fax machine sat on top of a short bookcase. The bookcase was filled to overflowing with philosophy textbooks and modern philosophical works of particular interest to me, along with all of Clive Cussler's novels, my guilty pleasure.

In my fax tray was a grainy photograph. A grainy *police* photograph, courtesy of Sanchez.

My stomach turned; I felt sickened all over again.

I carefully put the faxed photograph in a manila folder, grabbed my car keys and wallet from the desk's top drawer and left the office.

***

Huntington Beach was paradise. The best weather on earth. Few people would argue with me on that point. I drove south along the coast. Something must have been brewing off the coast, because there were some amazing sets crashing in. Alert Huntington surfers, or, rather, those with no life to speak of, were capitalizing on the gnarly waves. Dude. Their black forms, looking from this distance like trained seals, cut across the waves.

Two miles up the coast I turned left and headed up a small incline and parked in front of Huntington High. My home away from home.

It was 3:16 p.m., school was just out.

I moved up the central artery, past hundreds of yellow lockers, searching down row after row, until I spotted a janitor's cart parked outside a classroom.

***

Mario and I were sitting opposite each other in student desks that were entirely too small. My knees almost touched my ears. Desks seemed bigger in my day.

Mario was studying the photograph, not saying much. The scent of after shave, sweat and cleaning agents came from him.

Finally he looked up at me. "Yes," he said slowly, enunciating clearly. "That is him."

"You're sure?"

He nodded. "You killed him?"

I said nothing. He said nothing and looked away.

"He was a motherfucker," said Mario. "I am glad he is dead. He said he would kill my whole family."

"I know."

Mario pointed with a thick finger. "Someone

shot him four times in the chest. I would have shot him in his fucking face, too." He spat to the side. His lower lip was quivering. His accent was thick and heavy, his words now even more difficult to discern. "Why did he threaten my family? He is in hell. Straight to hell."

The thought of me sending Fuck Nut to hell was a bit burdensome. I decided to change the subject, somewhat.

"But the person who hired him is still free, Mario. We need to find him next. Do you understand?"

Mario nodded.

"Mario, what did you see on the night Amanda was murdered?"

I waited for him. His lower lip continued to quiver, and he seemed briefly unable to speak, but soon he regained some control of himself, and once he did, he told me everything.

And I mean everything.

60.

At 8:00 a.m., on a slightly overcast morning, I was driving south on the 5 Freeway with the windows down. My head was clear and empty, which was the way I preferred it. I had stayed off the booze for over a week and felt pretty good about it. I had had a good week of work-outs, even though my leg hurt like hell, even at this very moment.

To me the pain was worth it to play football.

The traffic out to San Diego was heavy but steady. At the rate I was going, I would be in

San Diego in two hours.

Two hours.

Despite my desire to keep my head clear, I thought about this aspect of traffic, and realized again I may have to move to San Diego if I made the team. If so, then I would see less of Cindy.

Not a good thing.

All to chase a dream I had given up on. A dream that had been taken away from me. It had been the dream of a young man, a twenty-two year old man.

I was now thirty.

For a fleeting instant the need to pursue an old dream, to re-hash what I had put aside, seemed sad and silly.

But it was the NFL, man. These were the big boys.

I had been on my way to the NFL. College ball had been surprisingly easy for me. I was a man among boys. Perhaps I thought more highly of myself than I should, but I had been pursued by the NFL since my sophomore year, and rarely has a day gone by that I had not wished that I had entered the draft sooner, prior to the injury. But I had chosen to stay in college. I had wanted my body to fully mature, to be physically ready for the rigors of the NFL. Mine was a demanding position, not as glamorous as some, but tough as hell.

At the moment, my leg was throbbing. Going from the gas to the brake pedal was taking a steady toll.

I shifted in my seat to ease some of the pressure.

I had taken three Advils this morning. The Advils didn't work, although my headache was long gone.

Was I good enough to make it in the pros?

Yeah, probably. College ball certainly couldn't contain me.

Traffic picked up a little. I entered San Diego county. Signs were posted along this stretch of freeway to be alert for illegal aliens running across the freeway, a picture of a mother holding a child, being led by the man.

I was thirty years old. I had moved on. I had a career as a detective. I was good at it. Hell, I even knew who killed Amanda.

A killer who needed to be stopped at all costs.

I thought of Cindy and our relationship. She had left me for a week, and then had come back to me. One of the hardest week's of my life. Too hard. Yet she had come back on her own, and I had done nothing to convince her that I was right for her. She had made that decision on her own.

Could I have made the NFL? Yeah, probably.

My leg would continue to throb every day of
my pro football career. Football was a twenty-
two year old's dream. I was thirty.

I thought of my mother and her own
unsolved murder.

There was much to do.

Time to quit screwing around.

At the next exit, I pulled off the freeway,
turned around and headed back the way I had
come. It was the start of a new day in my life. A
new direction. New everything.

My leg felt better already.

61.

On the way back to Orange County I pulled out my cell phone and made a few phone calls, one of them to Aaron Larkin of the Chargers. I left him a voice message thanking him for the opportunity, but I had decided to move on.

He returned my phone call almost instantly, furious. "Move on? What the fuck does that mean?"

"Means I'm not coming in."

There was a pause, and I knew he was thinking: *players would give their left nut for this opportunity.*

"I don't understand. Do you want to reschedule? I'll reschedule for you, Knight-horse, even though we have a whole crew out there waiting for you."

"I'm sorry."

"What happened?"

"Life happened."

"You could make our team, Knighthorse."

"I know."

"Don't do this."

"I have a killer to catch. Hell, two killers to catch. But for now, I will take one."

"What does that mean?"

"Means I have a job to do, and I'm good at it."

"This is the last time I'm asking, Jim. You walk away from this now and no one, and I mean *no one*, will give you another oppor-tunity."

"Good luck with the coming season. Go Chargers." I hung up, then called Detective Hanson of Huntington Beach Homicide.

62.

I arrived at Huntington High later that same day just as Mrs. Williams, the vice principal of discipline, was climbing into her Ford Excursion. The Excursion was raised an extra foot or two, and she looked miniscule sitting there in the driver's seat, adjusting her skirt. Her skirt rested just above the knees, exactly where most skirts should be.

I patted the fender of the Excursion. "You could conquer a small Baltic country with this thing."

"But could you take over a small Baltic country with *your* thing?" She glanced down at my crotch just in case I hadn't picked up on the innuendo.

I said, "Only if they were susceptible to fits of hysterical laughter."

She reached out and touched my arm. Her eyes were extraordinarily large at the moment. Green as hell. Or maybe blue. Hell, I didn't know. Her pupils were pinpricks. I could see the fine lines around her eyes and lips. She didn't blink.

"A big guy like you. I'm sure you're being modest."

"Mrs. Williams, are you flirting with me?"

"Oh, yes."

"Just as long as we're clear on that point."

"Oh, we're clear."

Her thigh was about face high. It was muscular, smooth and tan. She moved it toward me, and when she did her skirt rode up, showing more skin.

"You and I need to talk."

"Oh, we're going to do more than talk, sugar butt," she said. "Follow me home."

And so I followed her.

Sugar butt?

***

We drove south along PCH, through New-
port Beach and into Laguna. She drove quickly,
darting in and out of traffic, her need to see me
without my shirt on pushing her to drive reck-
lessly. Or perhaps she had to pee. Luckily the
Excursion was big enough to follow from outer
space.

She turned into a gated community, then
waited for me to catch up. When I had done so,
a pair of wrought iron doors swung open, and I
followed her in, passing beautiful Mediterran-
ean homes, each more elaborate than the next.

A garage door opened on my right and she
pulled the Excursion all the way into what must
have been a hell of a deep garage. I parked in
the driveway and got out.

The sun was hot on my neck. I was wearing
a loose Hawaiian shirt, jeans and black hiking
boots, although I wasn't planning on going for a
hike any time soon.

She stepped expertly down from the monster
truck and beckoned me to follow her through a
doorway that led into her kitchen. Once inside
she tossed her keys on a counter near the phone
and dropped her purse onto the seat of a dining
chair. I felt the need to toss something of my
own, but decided to hold on to my wallet and
keys. The kitchen was paved with tan Spanish

tile, and the cabinets were immaculate.

"Vice principals in charge of discipline do well," I said.

"Oh, they do. Especially for those who do their job well."

"I imagine you are one of those."

"Discipline is not something I take lightly, Mr. Knighthorse."

"I see. Does anyone oversee you, Mrs. Williams?"

"Dana, please." She took hold of my hand and led me out of the kitchen and into a much larger room. She hit the lights. "The answer is no one oversees me. Not really. If I failed to do my duties the school board would consider a demotion, but in actuality I am judge, jury and executioner at Huntington High."

"An interesting choice of words."

"Oh, I don't lay a hand on them," she said.

"But do you want to?"

"Always," she said without hesitation. "Some of them need to be beaten into submission."

"Do you have any children?"

"No."

"Good."

She laughed. "What would you like to drink?"

"Soda water is fine."

The room was very adult. There was a zinc-topped bar in one corner, filled with all sorts of alcoholic delights. Dana was there fixing us a couple of drinks. Off to the right was a large cigar box sitting on a delicate end table. Original artwork from local painters adorned the wall. I walked over to one and studied it. It was a stylized surfer hanging ten.

She walked over with my drink, took hold of my hand again and led me to a leather couch in the middle of the room. I sipped the soda water. She had spiked it with scotch. I didn't say anything, just set it down on a coaster on the glass coffee table. She was watching me closely.

"Do you like your drink?" she asked.

"It's very nice."

"I have never held the hand of someone so goddamn big before. Look at your hand, it dwarfs mine."

"You should see my feet."

"And you know what they say about that."

"I guess you could say I stepped into that one."

She giggled and drank deeply from her glass, then got up and made herself another. She seemed to be drinking something green on the rocks. Perhaps a Midori sour. She came back and sat closer to me. Our legs were touching. I was not aroused.

"How long have you been separated, Dana?"

"Does it matter?" she asked, leaning over and kissing my neck.

"Well it might should your husband use this moment to show up and make amends."

"Oh, please. You could handle him with one hand behind your back. However, he won't be coming home anytime soon. Does that put you at ease, sweetums?"

Sweetums?

"How long have you been separated?" I asked. "Six months? A year? Five years?"

She started unbuttoning my shirt. "Let's not go down that road right now, sugar butt."

As she reached for the next button, I grabbed her hand and pulled it away. "You're not separated are you?"

A small sound escaped from her lips.

"In fact, you are divorced, and have been from Bryan Dawson, current band director at Huntington High, for the past seven years."

"So what do you want, a fucking reward?" When she spoke, she glanced at the ornate end table. There was a small drawer within the end table. The glance was fleeting, then settled back on me. She leaned over and drank more of her Midori sour.

"Why did he divorce you?"

She shrugged. "You'll have to ask him that."

"I will. But I want to know why he divorced you when in fact *he* was the one cheating on *you*."

She shrugged again. "Apparently he was scared of my temper. Pussy."

"Why didn't you leave him?"

"It's called love, Knighthorse. I forgave him."

"But he was having sex with his students."

"None of us are perfect."

"You lived up north. How did you both end up here at Huntington High?"

She was sitting at the edge of her couch, her empty glass dangling from her hand. The ice cubes had a greenish hue to them. Her jaw was tight and rigid. There was a deadness to her eyes that might have been caused by the alcohol. Might.

"I came down first, once I realized the marriage was over. Tried to start over. I have a masters in educational administration. Never wanted to be a teacher, always wanted to someday work on the school board, where the money is. Because of sexual allegations, he lost his job up north, then couldn't find work anywhere. Said if he came down here and if I helped him get a job that he would go straight and we could start over again. I still loved him; the idea appealed to me."

"So you got him a job at your school?"

"Yeah. I had enough clout to push his application on through. There are some people who fear me."

"Imagine that."

"So he came down, hired on as a history teacher, and soon worked his way to band director. I was using my maiden name, and we kept things quiet about our divorce."

"But you started things up again romantically?"

She smiled faintly and looked away, looking back into her past. "Yes. It was nice. I felt the love again, you know. Real love. It was nice to have him back."

"Why do you claim to be separated, when, in fact, you are divorced?"

"Being divorced doesn't look good in my field. Makes you look unstable and less than desirable to oversee school policy." She got up and refreshed her drink.

"But then the allegations about Bryan started again," I said.

"Yes. The little bitches throw themselves at him."

"Is that what he tells you?"

"That's what I know. Have you seen him? Christ, he's good looking."

"A real treat to the eye," I said. "So you

blame the girls and not him?"

She turned on me, her drink sloshing over the rim and down her hand. "Of course I blame them."

"Amanda Peterson tried to leave Dawson, but he stalked her. Same with Donna Trigger. He stalked them relentlessly."

"That's bullshit."

"Amanda was seeing Derrick steadily. She considered her relationship with Dawson a mistake, but he would not let her go."

"Fucking bullshit. She was obsessed with him."

Her eyes darted around the room unsteadily, restlessly. She was twisting her hands in her lap. Her eyes repeatedly came to rest on the end table.

I continued, "I have a man, a certain janitor, who tells me he saw you put something in the back of Derrick Mason's car on the night of Amanda's murder. This janitor was later threatened by the same thug who threatened me."

She was breathing quickly. "Fucking nigger comes to my school, bringing with him his fucking nigger attitude."

"I assume you're speaking of Derrick Booker?"

"The fucking nigger."

"Yes, we've established that. Derrick loved

Amanda."

"Or so he says."

"What did you put in the back of Derrick's car?"

"Why would you believe I put something in his car?"

"Because the witness is credible."

"Maybe he doesn't like me."

"Hard to believe," I said. "Did you put something in the back of Derrick's car?"

She looked at me, and her eyes were alight with tears and something strange. Something akin to triumph. "The knife I used to kill Amanda. Killed two birds with one stone really. Got rid of the skank-whore and the nigger in one fell swoop."

I took in some air. I knew she had also hired the hitman, but that was a subject I was reticent to bring up, since the death of Johnny Bright was still an on-going murder investigation. The less said, the better.

"Why did you kill Amanda?"

"So she would leave my Bryan alone, the fucking skank-whore."

"Did you kill any others?"

She tilted her head and smiled. "Can you keep a secret?"

"Boy, can I."

"There was one up north."

"What was her name?"

"Tabitha something-or-other."

"You disposed of the body in the San Francisco Bay?"

"My my my, you are a good detective aren't you?"

"That's why I make the big bucks."

"Do you really?"

"No. Not really."

"So you just lied to me."

"It was meant to be witty repartee."

"I hate liars."

She spun away rapidly, reached for the end table drawer, yanked it open. I was at her side in three long strides. I lifted my foot and kicked the drawer closed just as her fingers curled around a revolver. She screamed in pain and frustration, turned and lashed out at me. I avoided the swipe, managed to keep my foot on the drawer, trapping her.

She clawed at my leg, but jeans are a wonderful thing: snug, tight and protective. Finally, she pounded on my poor injured leg until she sagged to the ground, whimpering.

We stayed like that until Detective Hanson, listening in on the wire strapped to my chest, burst in through the front door.

J.R. RAIN

63.

Stalking my pencil eraser was a black and white kitten.

It had white paws and a patch of white fur on its chest. It was slowly picking its way across my cluttered desk, around a Vicks Chloraseptic, over the latest James Rollins novel, and finally peering around my water bottle. From there it had a good view of the pencil eraser, which, coincidentally was twitching invitingly in my fingers. Now within perfect pouncing range, the kitten dug its hind paws into the grain of my pine desk, wound itself tight as a drum, then sprang forward, pouncing like a true champion. The eraser didn't stand a chance. The kitten and pencil rolled together across my desk in a furry ball of black and white.

My door opened, and in came defense attorney Charlie Brown and his faithful assistant Mary Cho. Charlie was bald as ever and Mary Cho's skirt still hung just above her knees. Nice knees. I looked up at her; she was frowning.

Caught again.

Charlie walked over and dropped an envelope on my desktop. The kitten pounced on the envelope. Charlie jumped back, surprised as hell that something on my desk actually moved. He straightened his tie and cleared his throat, tried his best to look venerable. When he spoke, he kept his eye on the feline just in case it should make an attempt on his jugular.

"A bonus," he said to me. "For catching the bad guy."

I looked at the envelope, which at the moment was feeling the unholy wrath of the furry critter. "You don't give a shit about the bad guy. Your client's free, and that's all that matters to you."

"I *do* give a shit, and I resent you saying that. That's slander."

"So sue me. Know any good attorneys?"

"Fuck you, Knighthorse. If you quit being such a hardass, I might throw you some more cases, seeing as you performed above expectations on this one."

"Flattery will get you nowhere, Charlie," I said.

He sighed. "Charles."

I picked up the kitten and thrust it toward the attorney; he jumped back, stepping on his assistant's toes, who stifled a scream.

I said, "Would you like to hold him, Charlie?"

"No, godammit. And it's Charlie. I mean Charles. Fuck." He turned and left.

"Assistant Cho, how about you: would you like to pet my kitty?"

"You're a pig."

When they were gone, I brought the kitten to my face and kissed his little wet nose. "What did I say?"

***

Cat Peterson left her abusive husband and she and her daughter moved in with her sister in a modest Spanish-style home in a city called Temecula, in a neighboring county called Riverside, a county made popular in many a Perry Mason novel. I pulled up in front of the house and, kitten in hand, walked up to the front door and rang the bell. As I waited, the kitten made every effort to kill my nose.

"It's been fun having you around," I said to him. "But you're going to grow up with a little girl now. You take good care of her, okay?"

He gnawed on my thumb, purring.

The door opened and once again I found myself staring down at little Alyssa.

"Hi," she said.

"Hi," I said.

"Tinker Bell ran away."

"I know."

"You know?"

I bent down and handed her the kitten. She gasped, then ripped the little booger from my fingers and hugged it with everything she had. The kitten, perhaps realizing that it had met its energetic match, submitted to the unabashed love. She twirled him around and around and dashed inside the house screaming for her mother to look at Tinker Bell Jr.

If ever a kitten was destined to be gay, it was Tinker Bell Jr. Of course, there's nothing wrong with that.

Footsteps echoed along the tiled entryway, and Cat Peterson appeared in the doorway. She was smiling, shaking her head.

"How did you know her cat ran away?" she

asked me, leaning a shoulder against the doorframe. There was a hint of a smile on her face.

"Might be better if you didn't know."

She nodded, suddenly somber. "I see."

I was motionless; she wasn't looking at me. Suddenly, and with surprising speed, she threw herself into my arms and thanked me over and over again for finding her daughter's killer. She didn't let go and I let her hold me and cry on me, and we stood like that for a long, long time.

64.

It was a rare spring storm.

Cindy and I were sitting together on my sofa, my arm around her shoulders, looking out through my open patio doors. The rain was coming down steadily and hard, drumming on my glass patio table. In the distance, above the rooftop of the restaurants, the sky was slate gray, low and ominous.

"You like this kind of weather," said Cindy.

"Yes."

"Why?"

"It's different. Don't you ever get tired of the never-ending sunny days?"

"No."

"Don't you ever think that it's nice for the land to replenish itself?"

"Only when you bring it up."

"Wanna walk in the rain?" I asked.

"I thought your leg hurt in this kind of weather."

"It does."

"But it's nothing like the hurt you've been putting it through these past few weeks," she said.

"I was blinded to the pain," I said, "pursuing an old dream."

"You're not blinded now?"

"No," I said. "The blinders are off. And now my leg just hurts like hell."

"What about your dream?"

"The dream was there for the taking. I didn't take it."

"Why?"

"People change. Dreams change. Life goes on. If I really wanted it, I would pursue it."

"So you don't really want it? Is that because of me? God, I feel horrible."

"Not because of you. When I was twenty-two, I wanted to prove I could play in the NFL. I wanted to prove I was tough enough. I had no other goals in life, no other conceivable ambition. Then, suddenly, I was forced to re-think and refocus my life, and I discovered that I could live without playing football."

"But you've always been...bitter towards being a detective. Because it was something your father did. It was something that caused him not to be in your life when you were grow-ing up."

"Father runs a big agency. I am determined never to be that big. But you're right, I was bit-ter towards my job. It was not my first choice. But then something happened."

"You discovered you were good at detect-ing," she said. "Damn good."

"Yes."

"What about proving yourself in the NFL?"

"Maybe some things are better left unpro-ven."

"But you think you could have made it?"

"In a heartbeat." I said. "Wanna go for that walk?"

"Okay."

I knew she didn't want to get wet, but she did it for me. We got our coats on. I grabbed an umbrella for her. I didn't mind getting wet.

Outside, in the rain, we moved slowly along Main Street. The shops and stores were all open, and a trickle of tourists, looking confused

at this unprecedented Southern California weather, moved past us. I heard one of them say:
"We can get rain at home."

"Can't please everyone," I said to Cindy.

"No."

"Want some chocolate?" I asked.

"Mmm, sounds yummy."

We ducked into The Chocolatiers. A massive
peanut butter cup for me and a sugar-free
almond rocca for Cindy.

"Sugar-free?" I asked, when we stepped
outside again.

"You can't taste the difference."

"Sure."

"Plus it's half the calories."

We sat down on a bench under an awning
and ate our chocolate and watched the rain.

"How's Derrick doing?" asked Cindy.

"His family is moving east. Hard to have a
normal life after being accused of murder. Kid
will be looked at differently, no matter how
innocent he is. UCLA is interested in giving
him a scholarship."

"Did you have anything to do with that?"

"I happen to know a few people there."

"So your work here is done?"

I looked away, inhaling deeply.

She reached out and placed her hand on top
of mine. It was warm and comforting.

"You're thinking of your mother," she said.

I kept looking away. "Her killer is still out there."

The rain continued to fall. She continued holding my hand. She squeezed it.

"You're going to find him," she said. It wasn't a question.

"I don't know what I will do to him when I find him."

"Does that worry you?" she asked.

"No," I said.

"Then it doesn't worry me."

65.

Jack was drinking a non-steaming cup of coffee. I was drinking a bubbling Coke. The dining room was empty. A very large teenage boy was filling some straw containers behind the counter. Minutes before closing.

I was toying with the scrap of folded paper.

"One thing I don't get," I said, turning the paper over in my fingers, "is why you always blow on your coffee. I mean, couldn't you just snap your fingers and it would be instantly cool? Or, a better question: how is it even possible that God could burn his lips?"

"That's more than one thing," said Jack.

"You're not going to answer, are you?"

He drank more of his coffee. His eyes were brownish, maybe with a touch of green. Maybe. What the hell did I know? I was colorblind.

"Could you heal me of my colorblindness?" I asked.

"Heal yourself."

"Heal myself?"

"Sure. I gave you a big brain for a reason."

"They say we're only using ninety percent," I said.

"If that much."

We were silent some more. I was thinking about my big brain...surely mine was bigger than most, since I was always being told I had a big head. Or were they referring to something else? I held up the folded piece of paper.

"I'm going to open this now," I said.

"Go ahead."

"I've wanted to for quite sometime."

"I'm sure you did, but you didn't."

"No," I said.

"Why?"

"Because I wanted to find the answer myself."

"And did you?"

"Yes."

The kid behind the counter walked over to us and told us we had five minutes. I said sure. Jack didn't say anything. And when the kid was gone, I unfolded the paper and looked down at the single word: *Dana*.

"Lucky guess," I said.

Jack laughed.

"So why did you come to me," I said. "Why are you here now?"

"You asked me here."

"Fine. Now what do I do with you?"

"Whatever you want."

"I'm thinking about writing a book."

"Good for you," said Jack.

"It's going to be about this case."

"Would make a good book," said Jack.

"I want to put you in it," I said.

"I'm honored."

"That is why you came to me, right?"

"That is for you to decide."

We were silent some more. The kid behind the counter was turning off the lights, banging stuff loudly so we'd get the hint.

"I feel we've only scratched the surface here," I said.

"That's why there's something called sequels."

"You mentioned something earlier about loving me."

"I did."

"So do you really love me?" I asked, a hell of a strange question for one grown man to ask another grown man. Especially a man as tough as myself.

He said, "More than you know, my son. More than you know." He reached out and put his hand on my hand. Radiating warmth spread through me instantly. "I am with you always. Remember that."

Something caught in my throat. "Then why do I feel so alone?"

"Do you feel alone now?"

"No," I said. The lights went out, and we got up together from the table. "No, I don't."

The End

Knighthorse returns in:
The Mummy Case
by J.R. Rain
Available now!

About the Author:

J.R. Rain is an ex-private investigator who now writes full-time. He lives in a small house on a small island with his small dog, Sadie. Please visit him at www.jrrain.com.

Made in the USA
Columbia, SC
17 December 2019

85163000R00207